# Wild Hearts Come Home

## A short novel by J S Morey

**Set in the grasslands of Wyoming celebrating the culture, history and legends of the Lakota Sioux**

**From the author of WILD HEARTS ROAM FREE**

# WILD HEARTS COME HOME
## J S Morey

First published in Great Britain 2023 ISBN: 9798396472952

**Further reading:**

The series 'Love should never be this hard':

Book 1: The Sign of the Rose
Book 2: The Black Rose of Blaby
Book 3: Rose: The Missing Years
Book 4: Finding Rose

Wild Hearts Roam Free – a modern western set in Wyoming

Unresolved? - a short story linked to 'Wild Hearts Roam Free'

Those Italian Girls – set in the hills of Tuscany

Read My Shorts – short stories and poems with a message
Three Easy Pieces - Easy to read short stories
Wood-Spirit - an anthology of poems about trees

For more by this author
visit www.newnovel.co.uk

# INTRODUCTION

As with all of my fictional works my aim is to introduce life values and circumstances for you to mull over with your own internal debate; to enjoy interesting storylines and characters - without making your mind up for you. Above all I hope to entertain as much as to inspire, not only using plot and characterisation, but also through context and location.

Context can be interpreted in several ways. As in most of my novels and short stories, context may simply be places where events take place. Or they may refer to a particular time period - usually the past - such as in my series 'Love Should Never Be This Hard'. Those four books span the mid-nineteenth to mid-twentieth centuries.

Invariably, that context is genre - the type and style of writing. In cases of romantic fiction, whilst I hope to satisfying the romantic reader, I try to steer clear of sensationalising love and relationships, or cheapen one of life's most seminal events. In so doing I rarely take you beyond the bedroom door.

Finally, I aim to address myth, legend and themes of a spiritual nature with sensitivity towards those who may hold strong views on certain subjects. Again, I hope to entertain without devaluing many people's strongly-held beliefs.

In short, just read for the journey on which I take you. Where you finally arrive is your business.

J S Morey

One more thing... treat *paragraphs that follow in italics* as illustrative, rather than part of the storyline.

# In the beginning...around 1965

Joss stood there astonished at such a preposterous notion.

'Dead? What d'you mean "I'm dead'?'

'Passed away.'

'So what am I doing here? Talking to you? Alive.'

'I called you.'

'You...?' Joss broke off, not sure what he wanted to say, clearly mystified as to who this stranger was in the first place – apparently *calling* him.

He paused, puzzled by the whole situation.

Finally he pressed for an answer. 'Who *are* you, anyway?'

'The Author. That's what you can call me. But my real name is God or, in some cultures - and particularly within some to which I will be taking you - The Great Spirit.'

The Author (aka a name that suits the All-Powerful) paused, conscious that Joss needed to digest what he'd just been told.

He would need time to decipher the mystery before him.

A minute passed – it seemed longer before Joss eventually spoke, accompanied by a stifled laugh – more of a snigger - from Joss, preceding his next question.

'D'you have any *proof* of that? I mean, I've *heard* of you, of course, but how do I know you *are* who you *say* you are?

'That you *are* God.'

Joss rested his case.

The Author responded immediately.

'What have you been taught?'

'About...?'

'About belief.' The Author was giving nothing away, asking him questions when it was Joss who needed answers.

'Faith?' There was uncertainty in his voice. 'You mean faith? Faith in what I believe?'

'So you *do* believe?' The Author asked.

'Yes. I suppose I do, or did, I should say, if I'm dead, that is.'

Joss' reply and particularly the confused and muddled way he seemed to be thinking, pleased the stranger.

'Good,' said The Author. 'Now we can move on.'

'Move on...? Move on to where....?'

'...the next stage.'

'The next stage of what?' asked Joss.

The Author answered by beckoning Joss to sit down next to him on the fallen tree in the forest. He had no idea how he got there, or from where he had just arrived. He simply revelled in the dappled light playing through the branches and leaves above, disturbed by a light breeze. It was warm, with a hint of freshness suggesting it was either early or late in the day, and late or early in the year. He took a guess, electing for the latter in each case, given that the sun's rays were not overhead.

It was the first time since meeting the stranger that he became aware of his surroundings, although he still didn't know *exactly* where he was. It was a clearing in a forest. From the absence of sounds other than those of nature, he determined it must be deep in the countryside and away from towns, villages or roads. There were no buildings – none that he could see – which was in sharp contrast to his last recollection of 'life'. It was certainly different from what vague recollections he *did* remember immediately prior to meeting...The Author.

The latter - his companion (for whom Joss was surprised at himself for thinking of in those terms so soon) locked him in a fixed gaze, almost mesmerising Joss to pay full attention to his next declaration.

'I'm sending you back,' The Author began. 'Straight back to pick up from where you ended up before you were... taken.'

'But who took me?'

Ignoring the unwelcome interruption at the risk of admitting it was him, The Author continued without apology.

'I did.'

'*You*...?,' Joss was stopped in his tracks as The Author raised a hand signalling him to cease - to 'not go there' - and to remain silent.

'It was a mistake. You were taken too early and I should have prevented it in the first place but, if you hadn't been pulled out *there and then* you would have made an even bigger mistake. I couldn't let you totally mess things up for yourself as it would have ruined things for the other person.'

'Ruined? Ruined what 'things'? And who is this *Other Person* anyway?' Joss had been allowed to speak this time.

He *did* need to know.

'Her name's Polly,' The Author replied, 'but that doesn't matter because you haven't met her yet... or... well... you have... but you're going to meet her again. For the first time... which will be the next time.'

'Does that make sense?' The Author paused.

He was aware - through Joss' strained look - that he wasn't doing too great a job at explaining himself. It was rare for him, as the all-powerful Author, to actually be called upon to do so; to be accountable to anyone else *but* himself. He cleared his throat as a precursor to beginning again, (hopefully) to make it much clearer this time.

Joss beat him to it.

'Reincarnation.'

'Re-?'

'-incarnation,' Joss burst out. 'That's what you're doing. Sending me back to begin again with... with this Polly. You say I'm dead, or maybe I was, and you're sending me back.

'I'll be alive again.'

The relief on the face of The Author was evident He followed up with a '*Thank you, Lord*' until he realised he was thanking himself. The hardest part was over – albeit no thanks to his own efforts. As they say, "nobody's perfect"... not that *he* of all people could admit *that*.

But the mere mention of 'Polly' triggered something inside Joss, opening a door to his memory, taking him to the *first* time he'd met Polly, and what had followed afterwards.

### *In case you were wondering about Joss...*

*Maybe this will help: I remember soon after our eldest granddaughter was born, a friend of ours saw her and said, 'She's been on this earth before.'*

*Hard to prove, maybe, but what if we* did *have a second chance, as it were? The first issue would be to establish whether or not you* remembered *events from your previous life, assuming you wanted to change their outcomes.*

*Our account begins with Joss, finding him in that - some would say fortunate - position, and being counselled by 'The Almighty', warning Joss not to mess things up this time.*

*Now I will hand you back to the story, one where things don't always turn out the way you want them.*

*No change there, then...?*

# Chapter One

Another Monday morning and the same routine lay ahead, starting at  8.17am - when the bus was due to arrive.

It was on time.

Joss boarded the double decker 'Midland Red' from his village, resigned to the twenty minute and five mile ride.

The same slow, predictable journey into Leicester.

'At least it's not raining,' he muttered under his breath. Not quietly enough it would seem. It prompted a nervous look from the girl standing next to him in the queue – the queue made up of the same familiar grey faces.

Expressions worn down by routine.

Joss responded with (aimed at the girl but to himself, silently), 'It's your own fault for standing so close. You trying to get fresh?'

Her look, on the other hand, was one that asked, 'Are *you* weird, or something? Talking to yourself?'

But he wasn't worried too much. She wasn't anyone he actually *knew*. Not personally. He knew *who* she was, knew her *name*, he even knew roughly where she *lived*. But that was as far as it went – as far as he wanted *to take it*, anyway.

Why?

You guessed it.

She wasn't much of a looker. Not up to *his* standard, which was the main reason he hadn't even tried to get to know her - all through the months he'd taken the same bus to work every day. But it had been suggested to him it was wrong *not* to make an effort to connect with people, even though you had no immediate reason to be friendly. Rewards would come later.

Leastways that was what his best pal had told him.

'You never know,' Trig had said, 'she might have a nice friend.' He was right, as usual.

It made him think of more reasons, like 'Or I might turn up one day without my bus fare and have to borrow from her.'

But he knew neither case was justified on this occasion. He just *knew*. He knew almost everybody in the village.

Apart from one girl – no, two girls in the village - all the others held no interest for him.

That wasn't true.

Further up the road in Glen Hills where '*the girl who  boarded at the next two stops along the line*' was concerned.

Now she *was* a looker.

That was how he described her to Trig because, of *all* people, *he* should know. He'd already dated two girls in Glen Hills, the posh area 'two stops further up the road.'

Simultaneously.

Yes. He would *definitely* be able to find out who she was, just as certainly as he could name every player and position of the Leicester City 1957 promotion side, despite the fact *that* promotion was now a ten year distant memory.

But in this case, at least *so far*, Trig had let him down. Even with *his* connections he'd yet to come up with a name for her let alone where she lived, assuming he *had* asked his current girl-friend to find out for him.

You see, Trig was lazy. He always delegated.

'Maybe he wants her for himself' Joss figured, 'given how frequently – and easily – he moves from one girl to the next.'

He was off on one of his day-dreams again, thoughts that kept him sane – or insane – depending on who you asked. It helped the journey pass more quickly - the same every day; the same stops picking up the same *people* - every day.

Two stops later the bus pulled in and his heart leapt.

Was she there? Waiting?

She was.

Smartly dressed (as usual) she obviously worked in an office, much the same as he did. Immaculately made up, but not in a cheap way, she was a real head-turner. Perhaps it wasn't an office she worked in after all but a beauty counter in a department store. Fenwicks – yes, maybe that's where she worked. The perfume would be a clue if ever he got close enough which, so far, looked like being never.

The bus was packed - as usual - with 'no room upstairs for the smokers' according to the conductor. She - the girl - made her way inside and downstairs, as normal, which is why he'd switched from being a regular upstairs passenger to taking a seat downstairs.

Every day.

He smoked, so he would normally go upstairs, but figured he could do without a cigarette for twenty minutes. She was worth that much, at least.

Back to the task in hand - getting close enough to talk to her - how could he guess *which row* she would take downstairs? Should he choose the front four rows in the hope she would grab the first free seat available? Or should he try further back, hoping she would look for a spare seat next to the window.

Or even the seat next to him.

Perhaps deliberately.

The bus moved off with a jolt. He wasn't ready for it and lurched back then forward, but he noticed how she held the overhead safety rail tight with her free hand, the hand not clutching her handbag. The forecast gave no rain that day so she didn't have an umbrella to worry about.

She began to move down the aisle.

'*Come on, come on, come on*,' he mouthed to himself, just his lips moving; no sound. He was *willing* her to take the seat opposite him, ideally across the aisle from him; not *so* close that they would be touching, but near enough so that striking up conversation didn't seem too unnatural or too strange.

Too presumptious.

Down the aisle she came. The guy in front of her looked like he would get to the empty seat opposite first until – as luck would have it – he spotted a friend on the back row and slid by Joss, so close his over-coat brushed Joss' face as he passed. He was in luck.

She sat down right opposite.

He found himself fascinated by how she held her coat modestly over her legs, looking about her as she settled into the seat. If she noticed him she didn't let on. Her handbag was resting on her lap protected by both hands. Palms down.

It was then he noticed she wasn't wearing a ring.

It was a good sign.

Also... was that a hint of a smile she gave him as she looked across, or just one of relief that she wouldn't have to stand for the journey? No. There was no smile. No acknowledgement, even though she *must* have recognised him from previous days. Mustn't she?

No. Not a chance.

She seemed oblivious to, looking straight ahead, looking forward at...what? Maybe it was to check out the same things on the journey and the same people who boarded every day; the same way *he* always did. For instance, there was this one very unusual scenario that played out *every* day that he couldn't quite work out.

It went something like this.

Before they reached the stop on the flat part of the main road through Aylestone there was a line of terraced houses with only small front gardens. Each had a gate apart from one. Instead there was a hedge, but quite a high hedge, high enough for a man to conceal himself discreetly behind it. There a single passenger usually got on; forties, wearing a trilby, navy blue gaberdine raincoat, shoes always well-polished.

And he was a smoker.

Joss called him 'smoker-man'.

He swore that 'smoker-man' and the bus driver, whoever that happened to be on the day, had a secret code: a signal for the driver to slow down for a pick-up, even though he could never see smoker-man waiting. He was hidden behind the hedge. Not even a glimpse. That was the strange thing; you never *saw* smoker-man. He wasn't visible to the driver as the bus approached the stop - not until the last minute.

But the driver always knew *when* to stop – and when *not*.

In advance.

Or so it would seem.

'Smoke signals, that's what it is,' Joss said – out loud and so unexpectedly it even made Joss himself jump.

'What?' replied the girl.

She'd naturally assumed he was talking to her. Joss was totally surprised, first at himself - that he'd spoken for all to hear; second that she'd presumed he was addressing her *and had replied*, as weird and as wacky as his own initial remark now seemed.

'Smoke signals?' she repeated.

'Yes.' He was emboldened by her question and felt that *not* to reply would be even more awkward. Even rude. He went on to explain fully. 'You see, that bloke in the trilby *always* pops out from behind that same hedge, the same garden hedge he stands behind out of sight almost every day, waiting, ready to get on exactly as the bus pulls up.'

'So?' The girl still couldn't figure it out. 'Smoke signals?'

By the puzzled look on her face Joss realised he was losing ground, so he had to think quickly.

'That's right,' he enthused, as if it was the most natural thing in the world for a person to do. 'You're spot on. The driver looks for smoke billowing out from behind the hedge as smoker-man...'

'Smoker-man?' Her expression became even more intense.

'That's what *I* call him, anyway,' he went on without faltering 'because he always has a ciggy on. Don't you see? That's what the driver looks for. Smoke...!'

He sat silent for now, waiting for her response.

'I...errr...think...so,' she hesitated. 'Either you're right or...'

'...or?' He stared into her eyes in anticipation.

'...or you're totally bonkers!'

This brought laughter from both of them as well as from one or two fellow passengers eavesdropping. But not from smoker-man. He'd already disappeared upstairs to carry on smoking now that a few seats became free. If only he knew, for one brief moment, he was the centre of attention.

'Joss... I'm Joss by the way,' he said.

'Polly,' she replied.

Then she came out with a question right out of the blue.

'So which detective agency do you work for?'

Now it was *his* turn to look puzzled.

'Nothing as flash as that, I'm afraid. Insurance. The Mercantile, in town.' He waited for her to digest the information, not sure whether she was impressed, disappointed, or... what?

'What made you think that?' he added.

'Oh, by the way you seemed to figure things out, and not in a normal way. Most definitely *not* in a normal way.'

She regretted her last remark and apologised.

'No. That's OK. I guess it *was* a bit off the wall,' he said. 'What about you? What do you do?'

'Guess.'

It was a challenge. He had to succeed now that he'd been described as being able to work things out.

'You work in Fenwicks.'

'How did you know?' she replied, surprised.

'It's on the label on your scarf. Your expensive scarf. You left the price ticket on.'

'Staff discount,' she answered, her searching look staying with him, either because she liked what she saw (Joss would always claim it was his blond hair and blue eyes) or...she was trying to figure out how come he was so smart.

'Did you think it was stolen?'

She flushed at her own self-accusation.

He didn't care.

Whatever the truth was, he couldn't believe how easily it was to talk to her – the girl who, half an hour before, he would have said was way above his pay grade. They continued chatting until they reached the bus terminus at The Newarke and the centre of Leicester. Now stationary they rose to shuffle patiently along the aisle to get off.

'I go this way,' He'd stepped down just behind her, at last close enough to notice her perfume. So close...

'We're on High Street.'

'I know,' she replied – a reply he *didn't* expect. So she *had* noticed him after all, even remembering the route he took.

'I'm this way, Joss. See you again, sometime?'

She turned to go.

'Tomorrow?' he called out as he watched her head towards Market Street in the opposite direction, adding 'Maybe?'

Too late. She was gone without appearing to hear.

### *So now we're getting to know Polly...*

*If you hadn't guessed already, Joss and Polly were made for each other. But would they share long life and happiness without too many bumps along the way? And which version - 'edition' - of Joss does she know?*

*Within all good matches comes inspiration for each, which is certainly true in our story. Even someone as blessed as Joss, with his good looks and charm - courtesy of his blond hair and blue eyes - can often belie an insecurity and surprising lack of confidence.*

*So many times such traits can only be overcome through inspiration derived from another - in this case from Polly.*

*With Polly and Joss, their connections with the past go deep. In Polly's case, her source of closeness stretches back to her evolutionary roots and heritage - in a place where she discovers her true sense of identity.*

*But how was that possible for a young girl swept along by  a modern-day life in a booming Midlands city in the 'white heat' of the rock and roll years?*

*You will have to read on...*

# Chapter Two

Amazingly, he realised he had a spring in his step, unusual for a Monday. He threaded his way through the side streets – the byways so familiar to him and steeped in history from the town once blessed by Richard III, centuries before. Some streets still retained the original narrow lanes - even the original cobbles, but for how long in this progressive city? It was a city that never seemed to stay constant from one year to the next. It suffered from a controversial mix of planning for future prosperity at the expense of abandoning past heritage.

Not to worry.

Today he was more absorbed by other thoughts; of her.

He went over and over again what they'd talked about – about her training in every department at Fenwicks, where she had started immediately after leaving school only a few months before. Joss was a year or so older and was recently promoted from office junior to trainee underwriting clerk, dishing out policies and dealing with minor claims. It was easy work and made easier still because he was in a small team – three in fact – about the same age as himself. They had so much fun during work hours, including the occasional game of darts in a nearby pub at lunchtime, plus plenty of overtime to earn extra cash.

She'd listened intently and seemed impressed.

He certainly hoped so.

But what about tomorrow? And the days after? Should *he* deliberately sit next to *her*? More to the point, would *she* sit next to *him*? Or was this just a 'one-off'? He didn't want to blow it just as he was so close.

But so close to what?

He decided to consult his best pal, Trig. Trig would know.

'You need a *reason* to talk to her again, that's if she doesn't simply plonk herself down next to you tomorrow,' advised Trig. 'Invite her to join you on something.'

'Like a date?' he asked.

'Not really. Don't make it such a big deal. If you make it look like a date then she has to commit herself one way or another as to whether she's interested in you. Or not.'

'Romantically, you mean?'

'Yes. So don't put her in a spot. Don't back her in a corner.'

Joss thought for a while.

'Maybe she'd like a game of darts at lunchtime.'

'You're such a plank at times, Joss,' Trig punched Joss' upper arm with a clenched fist, a knuckle protruding and therefore bound to make a bruise. 'You can't *ever* be serious.'

Trig knew Joss qualified on both counts. First he was serious; second, he was a plank.

'You're right, Trig. I'm bound to win at darts, which would certainly not go down too well.' Joss' face – the grin he couldn't conceal – gave him away, but Trig was far from pleased at being ridiculed.

'Fool!" Trig said. 'D'you want my advice, or not?'

'What about the Palais? Lunchtime? This Friday?' Joss' suggestion *was* serious this time. 'They have a two hour session – a disco – from twelve o'clock. It's only a shilling.'

Trig mulled it over for a moment before admitting, begrudgingly, it was perfect. He and his current girl-friend might even join Joss. 'I can get there for half past,' he said. Trig was a trainee sales assistant at a be-spoke gents' outfitters in the town and they shared the same lunchtime.

It was agreed – assuming Polly said 'yes'.

She did. That was on the Tuesday.

It was followed by sheer panic for Joss when she didn't show the following day, Wednesday. Nor on Thursday. Had she missed the bus on purpose? Was she avoiding him? Was she trying to get out of their arrangement (not a date) to meet on Friday lunch-time?

He had to wait until Friday *morning* to find out.

He was so relieved to see her, moving over as she took the seat next to him. He'd made sure it was va-cant. For the third day running he'd placed his briefcase *on* the seat next to him to deter others.

'Missed me?'

Her flippant remark struck him as odd, but in a good way. He didn't answer, not straight away, mulling over how surprisingly intimate – affectionate, even – her first words to him could be interpreted.

It made him wonder,

'Did they mean that *she* had missed *him* in the two days she'd been absent?'

He'd certainly missed her.

Why *had* she been absent? *Missing*?

'I've had a horrendous two days. Migraine. Doctor says I should go to the opticians in case I need glasses,' she explained. 'D'you think I'll need glasses?' She didn't wait for a reply. 'Hope not... they look awful on some people. Frumpy.

'D'you think they'll make me look frumpy?'

Joss replied before he even had time to *think* about it.

'Nothing could ever make you look frumpy,' he said. 'You're much too gorgeous for that.'

He looked round immediately in case anyone else had heard him, then turned back at her. She was looking straight at him but didn't say anything. The briefest of moments passed before she leaned forward, slowly, deliberately, until she was close enough to plant a kiss, softly, on his cheek. She lingered, their eyes just inches apart, her lashes gently brushing his skin.

Finally she spoke.

'That's so nice. Just what I needed to hear. Thank

you.'

'You're very welcome,' he whispered.

'I've really missed you, Joss,' she added. 'All I could think about were your beautiful blond hair and blue eyes.'

He took it as an opportunity to reach for her hand, instinctively, naturally, and before either of them could even realise. They passed the remainder of the journey in silence, joined together but savouring their own individual thoughts without trying to over-think the moment they'd just shared. The bus had arrived at the terminus, passengers already out of their seats and ready to disembark, before their spell was broken.

Polly spoke first. 'I'll try to make it for ten past one.'

Joss merely looked. 'Wha...?'

'This lunchtime. At The Palais? It's still on, isn't it?' A hint of uncertainty in her voice expected disappointment.

'Sorry. Yes, of course. Let's meet outside, or in the lobby if it's raining.'

He wanted to make it clear it was to be *his* treat, and he wasn't one of those cheapskates who came out with 'I'll meet you inside', to avoid paying. In any case, his official lunch hour was an hour and a quarter, starting at 12.45, so he was bound to arrive first.

Or so he thought.

Polly beat him by five minutes. She'd asked to

leave work a little early on the pretext that she had to go to the opticians, but she revealed the real reason to Joss as soon as she burst through the doors of the foyer of the Palais.

She really *had* missed him.

'I've been so looking forward to this,' she enthused. 'It's one thing that's kept me going these past two days. Dancing at lunchtime – what a treat!'

Joss wasn't quite so enthusiastic about the prospect of the actual *dancing* part, but he'd made the right decision in suggesting the right 'something'. It was the perfect choice. By the time they arrived the dance-floor was already packed, given that doors had opened at noon. By one o'clock it was at it's peak. Full or not, Polly wouldn't be deterred and, by the first few bars of latest Little Eva hit record 'Loco-motion', she'd already dragged Joss onto the floor.

It didn't stop there.

Polly insisted they get the most for their one shilling entrance fee by staying on for 'Breaking Up Is Hard to Do' by Neil Sedaka, followed by The Isley Brothers' 'Twist and Shout'. It was only when Bobby Vinton's 'Roses Are Red' began a slower set, that they left the floor.

'All that exercise has made me thirsty,' said Joss. They made their way to an empty table under the balcony. 'I'm going for a shandy, what can I get you, Polly?'

'Better make it lemon and lime, please,' she

answered, ' I can't really go back breathing alcohol over my customers.'

Luckily, they'd timed their exit from the floor perfectly; Joss was served straight away. He rejoined Polly with the drinks in the quiet alcove she'd found, quiet enough for them to talk. There was sufficient excuse for them to sit close together although neither had to shout above the music.

'Have you always enjoyed dancing?' she asked.

'I guess I have,' he lied, taking her remark first as a complement and then as an excuse to ask her out again, perhaps for the evening next time. 'I even had lessons.'

That was not a lie, since he and his pals – three others from the village – had tried ballroom dancing for a while, every Monday. Again, it was Trig who suggested it, saying they should all learn as one of the 'essential life skills' as he put it (goodness knows how or why he came up with that one), essential to growing up.

And for weddings!

They all went along with it, partly because it was a night they could all go out on the beer away from the same village pubs; in Leicester itself. The other reason was because they half agreed with him, realising rock and roll hadn't completely taken over at places like the Palais and the Trocadero ballrooms. Joss went on to explain more about his nights at the Castle Dance School.

'We all earned Bronze Medals a couple of months back – just for the waltz and the quickstep. Nothing to it, really. Next time we're going in for the Cha Cha and the foxtrot, although I'm having problems with that one.

'Do you dance ballroom, Polly?'

'Never tried it. You must teach me what you know.' He could see that she meant it. Right on cue, the first few bars of 'The Last Waltz' came over the speakers.

'No time like the present,' He stood up and offered his hand to her. Ignoring her weak resistance he led her to floor. By the time Engelbert Humperdinck had sung the final verse, some two minutes and thirty-odd seconds later, with Joss taking a strong lead they were dancing in perfect harmony.

'I knew you could do it,' he said as they stood together, motionless, still holding each other even closer now.


Did he make the first move? Or was it Polly? He couldn't remember as he was describing the scene to Trig later that evening. 'We just kissed,' he said to a 'trying-not-to-be-too-impressed' Trig. But he was clearly envious. 'It was like in the films. We just carried on, kissing until the next record.'

'What *was* the next record?' asked Trig, feigning interest and not really expecting a truthful answer.

He got one anyway.

'Moon River.'

'Which version – Danny or Andy Williams?'

'Danny.' Joss answered, wondering why it mattered in the slightest, but adding, 'then we got pulled off.'

'Pulled off *the floor*?' This got Trig's attention. 'Who by?'

'Some Mods.'

'Some Mods pulled you off the dance-floor? How come?' But Trig had guessed the answer.

'To make way for 'The Face'. The King of the Mods. He was there with his girl-friend and wanted the floor to himself.'

Joss went on to explain further. 'He had his Boys with him. Scooter Boys. Wearing Parkers. But *he* wore a full length leather even though it was quite hot, and he *looked* so cool. As did his girl.'

'So you all just let him take over?' questioned Trig.

'Like I said, he had his Boys with him. Anyway, he was good. They both were. They could really dance,' said Joss.

'To Moon River?' said a disbelieving Trig.

'Yes, to all two minutes twenty three seconds of it.' Joss knew this would annoy Trig. 'By Danny Williams.'

It did. Trig now looked irritated as well as incredulous. 'Two minutes, twenty sec.... ,' he paused. 'Joss, my friend, you need help.'


It was an event Joss and Polly would talk about for weeks ahead and, as he explained to Polly afterwards, he wasn't *totally* phased by it. It was just that he was so wrapped up in... well... her, really. You could say 'literally'. He had seen 'The King' take over the floor once before, the same guy but with a different girl. That time it had been at 'The Il Rondo', a haunt frequented by Mods. It had become the heart of the blues following and sometimes featured bands like The Who.

But it wasn't that event alone, at lunchtime, that had been such a game-changer; one that changed both their lives. Looking back they would wonder and marvel at the fact they had progressed from initial mild interest (on Polly's part, but somewhat stronger from Joss' perspective), to a growing fascination at so much mutual, common ground they shared, combined with a physicality that neither could understand.

Let alone control.

Basically, they couldn't get enough of each other. But even the strongest relationships can be threatened...and that's the time you need outside help.

From friends, family, or from The Author.

### Ahhh...love, lunchtime and Leicester all in one day

*They say 'you had to be there' when describing days and events of yesterday when everything was happening. Even the word 'happening' took over from the word 'occasion' to give special meaning to teenage stuff that was 'going down'.*

*Like other major cities, Leicester was swept along with the resurging economy, the 'white heat of technology' delivering new opportunities thanks to a progressive Labour government and - on top of all that - the arrival of The Beatles and The Mersey Sound. Even Liverpool football club was doing well. And so was Leicester City - reaching the FA Cup Final in the decade that was the 1960s.*

*The De Montfort Hall was bringing over American rock and roll bands and solo artists, supported by chart-topping British groups such as The Animals and girl sensations such as Dusty Springfield and Lulu. You could watch and dance to The Who at The Il Rondo blues venue and The Granby Halls - where I heard they played on seventeen separate occasions!*

*You could enjoy a lunchtime session featuring The Merseybeats in The Cavern, in Liverpool - for a shilling! And, for the same entrance fee, spend two hours dancing away to records at The Palais in Leicester; just like our Polly and Joss.*

*Of course, it all started in Britain with the 'Two I's' coffee bar in London - but Leicester had its own, too. One that youngsters would pile into at lunchtime would be just off the Clock Tower - I think, but I'm not sure - was down Church Gate. We would spend a lunch hour there drinking coffee from those clear perspex-type opaque cups and saucers, grab a cheese cob or a toasted tea-cake and, of course, keep the juke-box fed with sixpences so we could hear the latest chart-toppers.*

*It was fun; no overheads, no mortgage, no car even, but a job and a wage enough to finance our excesses.*

*Nightlife was just taking off in cities like Leicester, but not always fast enough, ending up with us piling into cars - for those of us lucky enough to afford one, for a night out in Nottinghma and Birmingham. If we stayed in Leicester, most night spots closed around eleven o'clock. From there we would seek out anywhere else still open that might grant us entrance.*

*I do recall some blues venue - no more than two floors of a terraced house to the rear of London Road railway station. It was run by newly-arrived Windrush immigrants from the West Indies. But our favourite, and one where we used to almost pressure the owner not to throw us out before one o'clock, was another coffee bar - this time off The New Walk or around there. I think it was called The Casa Marina or, simply, The Casa. That was followed either by a taxi or, most times, a long five mile walk home - weather permitting.*

*For some, the local culture could never provide enough entertainment and excitement. They would look for adventure further afield, often taking advantage of the £10 ticket to New Zealand, Australia, or Canada.*

*Polly and Joss chose a different destination, under different circumstances. However, the same goal was being sought - travelling a long, long way from home before discovering where they really belong.*

# Chapter Three

Was it really just three weeks ago that they'd first spoken, let alone started going out together – on actual 'dates'?

Yes. By Day 20 they were an item; boyfriend and girlfriend; 'going steady' as the Americans called it.

Seeing each other.

And why not call it that? They saw each other most days, if only on the bus to work every morning. For Joss it was the highlight of the day, especially as he couldn't always see her some evenings – but for good reason. First, he had night school on Mondays, studying for his insurance exams; second, on at least two nights he worked a couple of hours overtime.

Polly didn't mind; it showed her – and her parents – that he was ambitious. He was saving. Dare she ask what for? 'Best not,' she thought, 'not so soon.' But her parents were expecting otherwise. They liked Joss. Liked him a lot.

That led to their invitation.

'We must have that young man of yours round for Sunday lunch,' her mother suggested. 'It must be six weeks now since...and you still haven't even introduced him.'

So it was agreed. The following Sunday a scrubbed and polished Joss was walking up the driveway and ringing the front door bell of Polly's parent's. It was a detached house in the smarter neighbourhood of Glen Hills.

As he waited nervously in the porch he reflected on how his own parents' house didn't even have a doorbell, let alone a driveway. And they certainly didn't boast a gleaming new Shooting Brake parked in a double garage. But was he surprised at the sight? Not really. Polly had told him her dad was a doctor – a surgeon at the Royal Infirmary – which was way above the pay grade of his hosiery factory father. That differential alone added to his sense of trepidation and anticipation as he heard hollow footsteps approaching inside the hallway behind the freshly painted door.

He held his breath.

Relief followed apprehension as the welcome sight of Polly's gleaming white smile greeted him. She kissed him – functionally rather than with the usual passion – as she grabbed his hand to lead him into the lounge.

Their steps clattered in unison on the parquet floor-ing.

'Mum, Dad – this is Joss.'

At Polly's announcement her mother was first to rise from the leather Chesterfield sofa to reach for his hand. But then she drew him closer to plant an affec-tionate kiss on his cheek, followed by 'Goodness, Polly, you didn't say how handsome he was. If I were ten years...'

'Now Tara, behave,' interrupted Polly's father as he rose too from a matching armchair. 'And you'd better make that twenty years.' It was a joke that Polly's parents frequently shared and was followed by their laughter which, thankfully, was just the ice-breaker Joss needed to make him relax. So much so that his own reply surprised even him.

'I might have taken you up on it.'

'The boy has spirit!' her father added, grinning, much to Joss' further relief. 'Joss, you will have some wine? Do sit.'

'Yes, sir. Please.' Joss sat on the sofa, Polly close to him.

'Aran. Please call me Aran.' her father insisted. 'That's Aran with one 'a'. You may have guessed already, I'm not Jewish.'

Joss didn't reply, aware that the joke was intended, but uncertain as to how to respond.

'*This is where you need to be careful*,' uttered a voice – but a voice in his head which, without understanding *how* he knew, he took to be the voice of The Author. '*The last time you faced this situation you messed up, Joss*,' continued the voice, ' *but I will guide you this time. Have faith and you will know how and when to do the right thing. Try to relax*.'

'Are you OK?' whispered Polly when her parents were not looking. She'd noticed Joss' silence, but his demeanour had also changed; he seemed a little restless. Distracted.

He reached for her hand. 'I'm fine. Your folks are *so* nice!'

Polly accepted the explanation, sneaking a kiss behind his ear – with a touch of affection this time. But the sound of voice of The Author was still fresh in his mind, even though he was puzzled as to how he *knew* it was the voice of The Author. And how did he know *who* The Author was, now that he was so much 'of this world', with no recollection of anything that may have happened before? Messing up.

Aran's question brought Joss back to the 'here and now'.

'I know you're here for – hopefully – pleasurable reasons, Joss, but may I ask your help on a matter of... business?'

Joss was still wondering what this 'matter of business' was, when Polly's father satisfied his curiosity. 'You will have seen my new shooting brake out in the driveway,' he continued. 'Is there any chance you could quote me for comprehensive cover? Polly tells me you're in insurance.'

As an employee at The Mercantile, Joss had a staff agency where he was able to earn a discount on any insurance he introduced, for which he was able to pass on to friends and family discounted terms – in this case 15%.

'Why, yes, of course,' he answered. But that was before he realised one massive obstacle in this particular case. Before he could carry the conversation further the voice in his head – that of The Author – broke in. '*Think carefully, Joss. This is where you went wrong the first time. Consider your priorities. You don't want to lose Polly, now do you*?'

It was Aran who spoke next. 'My existing insurer is not actually refusing to insure the Brake, but the premium is much, much higher than it had been for the Humber Super Snipe I had with them. And it carries a £50 accidental damage excess. I'm not short of money, of course, but it's the principle. It seems so wrong. It's almost as if they are penalising me because of what I am.'

Joss knew exactly what he meant. He'd fallen in love with Polly without any consideration of her ethnic background. For him and his generation, the growing population and presence of Asian families was a simple fact of life. He had friends and classmates who were Indian by birth and he considered it all part of everyday life. Normal.

The problem would be with The Mercantile.

They had rules.

Joss recalled the many times he was called to the counter at the office whenever a 'walk-in' – a casual enquirer – would appear and ask for insurance cover; only to be refused.

'I'm sorry, but we do not accept black people. It's company policy.' He could hear himself saying those very words, forced upon him by The Mercantile, written into their instruction manuals even though he knew, in his own heart, it was wrong.

'But I'm a British Citizen,' the shocked enquirer

would say.

Joss would then have to stand his ground, protecting 'the company' – a company that also had market traders, gypsies, travelling salesmen, and publicans, on the same rejection list.

Ironically, you really could call it a 'black list'.

Today, in the case of Polly's father, he decided to make a stand. You could say, 'The things we do for love.' But how would he get Aran's application through, for his insurance to be accepted? He had no idea right now, but the main thing – you could say selfishly and self-servingly he *had* to do - was to succeed in getting the cover for Aran at all costs.

Otherwise it would be a betrayal and he could lose Polly.

There were no more voices in his head; not that day. (He joked to himself later that even The Author needed a day off.) Luckily he was also able to disguise his inner turmoil caused by the daunting task that lay ahead. Taking an instant liking to Polly's parents helped. Lunch proceeded with a surprisingly amusing injection of banter from Polly's father. Combined with a level of graciousness from her mother, it coated the whole proceedings in a cloak of warmth that he had only witnessed previously at his own parents' home on similar occasions, or at family gatherings with aunts and uncles.

The meal was splendid and it strengthened his resolve to invite Polly to *his* house at the earliest opportunity.

'I'll have to come back to you on Tuesday with a proposal form to complete,' Joss explained as he was leaving. 'Then I can get a quote for you by Wednesday.'

He would normally have done so on the next day were it not for his evening classes on Monday.

That will be fine, young man,' Aran answered, shaking Joss' hand warmly before Polly's mother stepped forward to embrace him affectionately. Polly took over, volunteering to walk Joss to catch the bus for his return journey home.

'I'm so proud of you,' she said, leaning into his side as they walked the few yards, slowly, to the main bus route.

'What for?' He really didn't feel he'd done anything so remarkable to deserve such praise.

'You've always treated me... well... like you would have had I not been...' She paused.

'Asian?' he asked.

'I've never really thought about it,' he replied honestly. 'Not until now. With the insurance thing and discrimination against non-whites, it's all so false.'

'It's just human nature,' she replied. 'and I have to admit something to you.'

'What...?'

Polly couldn't hold back now, but her voice trembled as she began to confess. 'I very nearly didn't go out with you because you're white. I was worried –

not for me – but for what people would say *to you*. And about you, *because* of me.'

'I don't care about other people.' Joss stopped, turning to her so that she could see his face – so she could be sure he meant what he was about to say. 'I had no doubts about you or my feelings for you. The way your parents treated me today has made me even more certain, if that were possible.'

There was no voice in his head today but he was still conscious of The Author's previous advice – *not to mess up this time.* Joss continued. 'This insurance thing. I'm going to get it done even if it's the last thing I do.'

It was – it was *the last thing* he did at The Mercantile.

Joss had the authority to issue – to 'write' – policies, as an underwriting clerk. Once he'd collected the completed, signed proposal form from Polly's father he made out the contact document himself, rushing it through the typing pool at its most busy period so that, even if the supervisor saw the policy document, she hopefully would overlook any hint that, by the letter of The Mercantile code of practice, it had been issued without the required counter-signature by Joss' head of department – the Chief Clerk.

To expedite matters, Polly's father paid the premium through Joss, thereby avoiding a 'personal appearance' by Aran at the office and, therefore, more suspicion. Once issued there was no going back – not for The Mercantile. The contract was now bound by Common Law. Everything had gone so smoothly. That was until the end of month figures were issued.

'Close the door behind you, Ryan,' said the Chief Clerk as Joss entered his office. He'd been summoned as soon as the list of new policies had landed on his boss' desk. One name had been ringed in read, followed by an exclamation mark. That name was 'Patel', followed by Joss' – 'Ryan' - underlined as being the agent who'd introduced the new customer.

The new *Asian* customer.

But it was too late for The Mercantile to detract.

'How do you explain this, Ryan?' seethed the Chief Clerk as he pushed the report across the desk. It slid on the lacquered surface and came to rest directly under the nose of Joss.

'British Citizen, top surgeon in his field, clean licence, no previous accidents... .' Joss recited, pushing it back.

'...called Patel?' exploded the Chief Clerk.

'...so?' replied Joss, doing his very best *not* to sound insolent, but failing.

'So? So he's black – and you know damned well our rules against....his kind.' The Chief Clerk's last expletive was too much for Joss – he couldn't hold back this time.

'With respect – *sir* – "*his kind*" could potentially

save your life if you ever needed – heaven forbid, because it's the last thing I hope you will need – heart surgery.'

'You don't seem to get it, Ryan. He's...'

'...a black man. Yes. I know. And a very fine *black man*, if I may be so bold.'

The Chief Clerk was caught between common sense, what he knew was morally right, and 'the corporate line' as it were – the edicts laid down for him to follow. And for Joss. There was no real way out for either of them, so each went along with the path already prepared for them.

'I think it'll be best all round if you leave,' the Chief Clerk announced, straightening himself in his chair to emphasise the gravity of the step he felt compelled to take.

Joss said nothing. Any word or protest from him at this moment might just weaken his position; it might just come over as a capitulation of *his* position – or an apology.

The Chief Clerk made it quite clear what *he* wanted.

'It's the start of a new month but I still want you gone immediately. No need to work your notice. By the time the bean-counters in London have seen what you've done and how you've contravened company policy, it will be better for me if I can say you've already left the company.

'I'll pay you until the end of the month as well as

granting you a month's pay on top. All I need is your resignation and I can begin the paperwork. I'll provide you with a reference but don't expect any accolades for past achievements, even though I do feel it's a shame you've sullied a lot of the progress you've made over the last two years. I saw great things for you.

'So goodbye and good luck, Ryan.' He paused, softening his tone now the difficult part was over.

'Joss.'

Joss took the Chief Clerk's outstretched hand with a solemn – but not sullen – 'thank you', in gratitude to the quite generous severance package he'd been granted. But then he remembered he had holiday pay... but he was cut short with a 'Don't push it, Ryan.'

He left immediately, packing up what few personal belonging he had in his desk before telling his workmates – he limited this announcement to just four colleagues – inviting them the pub next door for a farewell drink after work. He would wait until he saw Polly the following evening before he told her. By strange coincidence it was when he planned to deliver the policy document to her father for the car insurance – the very instrument that had landed him in this position.

But he had no regrets. Instead he felt a relief; a freedom tinged with fear.

# Chapter Four

The hardest hit by the news was Polly.

Distraught - guilty even - that he'd virtually sacrificed his job and career just to help her father, Polly's first reaction was to explain everything to Aran in the hope that he could at least do...something. Something to reverse the situation; to have things back to how they were.

But Joss would have none of it, making her promise that she would keep the real reason he'd left The Mercantile to herself. He'd vowed to always be honest with her; and he was. But what story should he make up for her parents whilst, at the same time, making sure he wouldn't lose face in their eyes. The last thing he wanted was for Polly's dad to surrender the insurance policy Joss had so expensively 'won' for him. That's what it felt like for Joss – a win against all odds. No. That musn't happen, otherwise it would have all been for nothing.

He quickly put a plan into place.

First he needed a source of income to sustain the kind of lifestyle he was used to – he needed to pay his way, keep himself clothed and fed, and make sure he and Polly could 'carry on as usual' until he decided on his next step. Perhaps even *their* next step. He'd made up his mind to take pretty much any job within reason. He explained all this to Polly; he'd told his own parents soon after, but decided against telling Polly's parents. It would only make them worry. Most of all he didn't want them to feel guilty or responsible in any way for what had happened.

Then he had a lucky break.

Ted was a team-mate in the soccer side he played for on Sundays and worked for the local brewery. He was a supervisor who oversaw the work-force in the bottling plant. They were hiring. The work involved long twelve hour shifts which, if they weren't hard graft they were monotonous. It wasn't a job with many prospects but the pay was good or, at least, better than he'd earned at The Mercantile.

It was perfect. He could even save. It also bought him time – time to decide what he *really* wanted to do.


'Your hands are so rough,' Polly remarked on one of the few evenings they had together. He'd been pulling double shifts which ate into his leisure time – *their* time.

'So you want me to wear gloves when we...?'

'No, Joss. That's not what I meant.' Polly was upset in case she'd offended him. The job he'd taken was well below his ambitions but she was proud of his work ethic.

'It's only until I get things sorted out. I promise.' She leant forward to kiss him. A 'thank you' showing she supported him. It would give him time to decide what he *really* wanted. What he wanted *for them*.

Sometimes fortune smiles when you least expect it.

Although it wasn't in Joss' overall plan, nine months down the line saw Joss still working in the brewery but in a different role. The tedium of the bottling plant was replaced by something a lot more interesting. He was drafted into the team actually producing the beer itself – for casks as well as bottles. The hours were still long but the impact on his body – and particularly his hands (!) - were less. Shifts passed more quickly and it was interesting work.

He was learning a trade.

He even made friends – workmates – which made the job even more fulfilling. The Asians with whom he grafted on the production line were not particularly chatty; but they were pleasant to him in a passive way. Even so he admired their commitment to hard work and their long hours, with rumours that they shared 'hot beds' with fellow workers on different shifts. Discrimination against them was, at times, quite blatant, which made him feel some degree of satisfaction that he'd been able to balance the books, albeit in a small way. By obtaining justice for Polly's dad he'd made a difference - even though he ended up being sacked.

One friend in particular at the brewery brought him both companionship as well as opening the door to a new career – a new life, even - one for both himself *and* Polly.

But it was four thousand miles away.

'I recognise the accent, but what part of America are you from?' Joss asked as the 'new guy' joined his team.

'Wyoming. Casper to be exact,' the new guy – Jonesy – answered. 'My dad's posted here at the American air base just outside of town.'

The 'town' to which Jonesy referred was the city of Leicester, of course. The aerodrome was Bruntinthorpe – more than just 'outside of town but Joss noticed Jonesey had 'wheels'. Not just any old 'wheels' but the open top TR4a that virtually all the American personnel seemed to own – much to the disgust of the locals.

They could barely afford a beat-up Morris Minor!

'It's my dad's,' explained Jonesy as Joss stood admiring the sleek lines of the sports car. 'He visited their factory in Coventry and just had to have one.'

'Just like that?'

'Just like that,' Jonesey confirmed.

'How come you ended up here?' Joss was clearly envious and keen to change the subject.

'Oh, I worked for the local brewery company in Casper. That's where I got my experience.' Jonesy had made it all sound so easy but Joss began to think. He had the start of an idea which grew the more he learnt about the brewing process; and the more he became friends with Jonesy.

With his good looks and apparently unlimited supply of money, Jonesy was never short of female companionship. That was another irritation for the locals. The downside was that Jonesy occasionally turned up to work with a black eye or cut lip. Locals in his village made their irritation known in many visible ways.

But he and Joss got on well, often making up a foursome. The TR4a was able to carry four – at a pinch. During one such outing the conversation got around to 'what do you want to do with your life, Joss?'

'S'funny you should ask,' Joss replied, casting a glance towards Polly as he went on to explain, conscious he'd not discussed it with her beforehand. 'I've been thinking of doing what you've done. But in reverse.'

'How's that work?' a puzzled Jonesy replied.

'Yes... how...?' Polly began, a little peeved that he'd yet to share it with her. Joss cut her short with an apology.

'Sorry, Polly, I know I've not spoken to you about this but I've only just had this idea.' Joss took a deep breath.

'Why don't we go to America?'

'To Amer-...?'

'Yes, Pol. To Wyoming – Casper to be exact.' That certainly got Jonesy's attention. He was straight back in.

'You're talking about the brewery company? Taking my...'

'...your *old* job,' Joss enthused. 'You said they'd take you back anytime. That means there must be a job waiting.'

'Yeh, well, I guess so.' Jonesy thought for a while then was soon up to speed. 'So you want me to...'

'...find out *for me*'. Joss finished Jonesy's sentence yet again then sat, silently, waiting for a reaction. Hopefully a 'yes'. But Polly spoke next, her voice faltering as she choked back the tears. In his head, and unheard by the others, Joss could now hear The Author sigh in exasperation at Joss' lack of tact. Both He and Joss were fearful of Polly's reaction.

'You mean you're... leaving me...?'

'No, no. I would *never* do that. We go together. What d'you say, Polly? It would be an adventure!'

He looked patiently for her answer but her slow reaction was too long for his liking, until...she turned to face him.

'Why, yes. Of course.'

She went quiet so she could think. Joss heard - almost felt - The Author as he exhaled in relief, having held his breath and fearing the worst from Polly.

'But what would *I* do? I know nothing about beer.'

Luckily, Jonesy had the answer.

'I can get you a job in the office. You can type, can't you, Polly?'

Joss and Jonesy – and Jonesy's girlfriend - were

now staring at her, waiting. It had to be the right answer.

'Of course I can type,' Polly said much to their relief, demonstrated by smiles all round as if Polly had just passed an exam. Or so it seemed at the time. More than that, did it mean she and Joss were *definitely* going for it? What if her answer had been 'no'? Would it have scuppered the whole notion of picking up sticks and starting a new life? What *had* she signed up for – without even knowing the fate waiting for them out in the strange land? Events that would change their lives.

Forever?

### *The post-war American invasion*

*Jonesey would have appeared so privileged to Joss and Polly, as did all Americans and their affluence compared to a Britain still paying for the war - for decades after. Paying back the loan we needed to build and buy tanks, guns, ammunitions and aircraft, amounting to billions - our debt to America.*

*America gave us rock and roll...and then some. Through films and music our own youth were filled with desire - desire to own the fancy cars, homes graced with refrigerators and inside toilets and, above all, with television.*

*Life in America was seen as 'fast', whereas Britain was 'slow', although that would change, albeit some fifty years later.*

*Life for the Native American Indian was a life in the slow lane, partly at the hand of 'white America' and leading to poverty and a poor standard of living and opportunity for indigenous tribes, but also because in many ways the latter didn't wish to embrace 'the fast lane', rejecting materialism in the hope that spirituality would sustain them in a more honourable way.*

By the following Tuesday it was virtually a done deal. Jonesy had leapt straight into the task of securing Joss and Polly a job each – at least in principle. What Jonesy hadn't admitted was that his dad was part-owner of the brewery and had made calls to the managing partners. That guaranteed Joss a place. They created a job for Polly in administration combined with working in the tap room – the bar that fronted the factory.

Visas and permits would have to be sorted out on arrival - strictly 'off-book' as it were.

Breaking the news to family was the harder part.

Telling Joss' parents was straightforward. They were delighted he'd finally found an avenue for his ambition. That was obvious from the enthusiasm with which he described his new 'career move'. As for Polly and her parents it was not so easy to present a plausible story – to explain why it was *so* important to leave the bosom of the family at such a young age, venturing into the wide world *with no chaperone*. But

Mr and Mrs Patel were 'modern thinkers', deeply integrated into their adopted western culture. After the initial shock they realised where Polly's heart lay.

First and foremost it lay with Joss.

The Patels had the same confidence and trust in Joss as did his own parents. 'This will be a grave shock to her mother,' Mr Patel - Aran - said, referring to his wife. Joss had just announced his intention to whisk Polly of to the unknown in a matter of a few short months.

'Have you both thought it all through carefully?'

'Very much so, sir.' Joss' reply wasn't a complete lie, although it had been just over a week since he and Polly had actually both taken on board a notion that had, at first, pretty much emerged out of the blue. Since then they'd talked of nothing else, making plans, waking up each day filled with excitement at the prospect of adventure in the 'new Wild West'.

There was still another surprise awaiting Polly.

'I was hoping that Polly wouldn't be leaving home until she was married.' Polly's mother had been sitting quietly listening to Joss and Aran talk tentatively about this sudden 'new arrangement'. She could hold her silence no longer.

'I would like your blessing on one other aspect,' said Joss, straightening up as he spoke, as if ready to make a major announcement which, indeed, he was.

'*Be very careful what you say next!*' It was The Author, the deafening voice in Joss' head making him start with surprise. '*Your actions now, and what you are about to ask, affect more than yourself, young man. Other lives will have to bear the consequences if you are wrong.*' Joss could almost taste the urgency in The Author's tone.

'Is anything wrong, Joss?' Aran Patel had noticed the change in Joss' composure. Had he been listening? Could he hear?

'No. Not at all,' Joss reassured him. ' It's just that...I would like her hand in marriage. Your daughter, I mean. Polly. I want to marry her....'

He paused, before adding. 'Please.'

He waited.

Relief on Joss' face was obvious when Aran and Tara burst out laughing – a joyous laughter – with, 'Of course you have our blessing, doesn't he, Aran?' In a way he was glad it was Tara who responded first – and so positively. Aran embraced his wife as confirmation he agreed with her totally.

'What did Polly say when you asked her, Joss?' asked Tara, grasping both his hands and holding onto him as if she was fearful he would get away.

'Ummm...I... errr...well, I haven't asked her yet,' he said.

A further pause from Aran and Tara followed before they exploded into another bout of laughter – this time almost uncontrollably. Was this boy for real?

'*You seem to be winning, young man,*' came the voice of The Author. '*This time you're not disappoint-*

*ing me. Not so far.'*

The last three words brought Joss back to reality – the reality that Polly might still refuse him.

'*She wouldn't, would she?*' he questioned himself, silently.

'You'll be fine,' came Aran's reply. His wife agreed.

'I'll fetch her. She was getting ready before you arrived and must still be upstairs in her room. Probably listening to us.'

With that Tara left, her footsteps clear on the stairs leading to the upstairs landing above them.

'Sit down, Joss,' said Aran. 'We have lots to plan. Have you any idea of a date? A month, at least.'

'That's it, I'm afraid,' Joss dreaded this part. 'It will have to be soon if we are to be married before we leave.'

'Oh...' The single syllable and the silence that ensued spoke volumes, as did the disappointment on Aran's face at the news. How would he explain this to Tara? Traditionally – culturally – weddings for his faith were arranged well in advance, included family and extended family and friends, and lasted several days. Clearly this Christian boy had no perception of what was expected. Tara returned to say that Polly would still be a few minutes before she joined them.

'Tara, my dear,' Aran announced, a hint of mischief in his eyes, 'I think we'll have to dispense with the elephant.'

Joss stared at Aran in disbelief.. '*Had he gone*

*mad?*'

Then Tara stared – but at Joss, not Aran. She knew *exactly* what Aran was talking about. She gasped, to all intents and purpose upset at the revelation.

'Oh no. A wedding without elephants?'

Joss remained puzzled at Tara's confused look. Had she, too, joined the craziness?

'Elephant? No elephant?' she repeated. 'How will Joss get to the wedding with no elephant?'

A weak apology for a smile – the smile that says '*I think I know what they're talking about, but I'm not sure,*' told Aran and Tara they owed Joss an explanation, sooner rather than later and before Polly came down. Aran and Tara were hugging each other in mock consolation, intermittently breaking into laughter and smiles. Joss had never seen them like this.

'I'm sorry,' admitted Aran. ' We're not laughing at you. Not *really*. Let me explain. You see traditionally – *and if we have time* (was Aran trying to make a point with this last remark?) – we arrange for the groom to arrive at the wedding ceremony *on an elephant.*'

They stood silent again, waiting for Joss' reaction.

'*Did he understand?*'

Eventually it dawned on him. His smile changed into quiet, subdued laughter – but laughter all the same – as he recalled photographs he'd seen in the Leicester Mercury. Pictures of a Hindu wedding with the groom mounted on a decorated elephant. He breathed a sigh of relief but, stumbling over his words confessed, 'I'm not too good with heights.'

'Don't worry, my boy,' Aran replied, 'A taxi will have to do – perhaps my Shooting Brake, given that we owe it to you that it's on the road again and safely insured. I think it would be most appropriate, don't you, cocking a snoot at those Mercantile people where you used to work?'

'I wouldn't be able to pay you,' Joss replied. 'That's not covered by the insurance,' to further laughter. Then it dawned on him, '*Who had told them the real story why he'd left The Mercantile?*'

That question would have to wait as Polly appeared.

'You all seem to be enjoying yourselves.' She glanced from face to face before settling on Joss, her expression alone told him she wanted answers.

'I think Joss has something to ask you,' Tara announced. 'Come on, Aran, we'll go into the kitchen while they talk.'

'Talk? Talk? What's going on?' Polly grew nervous.

'It's good news,' said Joss. 'I hope.'

'News? What news?'

'Your parents have agreed.'

'Agreed? Agreed to what?' She was even more nervous.

'Sorry, Polly. I mean, as long as you agree.'

'Agree to...?'

'...to marrying me. Will you? Will you marry me?'

Polly paused for a while – too long, Joss thought.

Finally she spoke: 'Shouldn't you be on your knees?'

'I'm sorry...I...'

'Just kidding. Joss, of course I'll marry you. What took you so long?' She flung her arms around Joss in pure delight.

The door to the lounge burst open, Tara first then Aran, spilling into the room to embrace first Joss, then Polly.

Of course they'd been listening at the door.

'It's fortunate you said yes, Polly,' said Aran. 'Your mother has already booked the hall five minutes ago.'

With that Tara went back into the kitchen, returning with a bottle of sherry and four glasses. 'This is purely medicinal,' she warned as she set about pouring four glasses. Joss had heard stories before about Hindus not consuming alcohol, but the Patels were 'modern and progressive'. Even so, he was surprised that Tara felt she had to apologise for her apparent breach of the cultural code. And he hoped it didn't *taste* like medicine.

They made a toast. Tara and Polly were in tears - of joy - with Aran not far behind, trying to control a sniffle.

### Aran and Tara - a gift of good parenting
*Parents teach us so much by example, even*

*without meaning to, instinctively, and without thanks or reward. At the time.*

*Polly's parents are no different here. Their positive influence is felt doubly so, helped by their example of succeeding against adversity and prejudice, as well as their acceptance of change and working twice as hard to obtain the best from life.*

*Above all, gifts of this nature bestowed on one's children last a lifetime.*

# Chapter Five

A few weeks later Polly was in tears again as they finally waved goodbye to her parents at Heathrow Airport.

Tara was insistent on leaving it to the very last minute before she was to see her beloved daughter for the very last time, at least for some time to come. Joss and Polly – and Tara - had travelled in style in the Shooting Brake. The M1 motorway down to London, where they had joined it at Crick just south of Leicester, had been open for five years or so. It was the first time either of them had experienced motorway travel. Aran was cruising at 85 miles an hour but remained vigilant for speed checks since the introduction a few months earlier of the 70 miles per hour limit.

They felt like royalty sat in the back seats. Polly gripped Joss' hand for the whole journey - the hand sporting her new wedding ring. Leaving home was a big step for her.

They'd bought *return* tickets on BOAC Airways partly for Tara's peace of mind (but with no resistance from Polly – or Aran), and partly to avoid suspicion from the American immigration authority. It would prove to passport control that they intended to return to the UK, and disguised the fact they would be working during their stay. They'd given Jonesy's uncle's address as where they would be staying.

That wasn't a lie.

He'd offered them a home for as long as they needed it, even though their intention was to find their own accomodation as soon as they'd settled in to the job. Her uncle would help them with work permits if and when they decided to make their stay more permanent – their original intention.

Polly was waving out of a window again – this time the window of the aircraft, peering towards the airport terminal from which they'd just taken off. She couldn't *see* her parents but she *imagined* them waving from the viewing lounge overlooking the runway as they took off.

She was right.

Once 'her children' were airbourne, Aran comforted his wife, coaxing her back to the car for the journey home.

This time minus two.

Tara could already feel the hole left by Polly's absence.

'With every minute that passes she is seven miles further away from us,' she said tearfully as they rejoined the motorway for the final leg home.

'Don't torture yourself, Tara.' Aran released his hand from the steering wheel to hold hers. 'She will always be in our hearts and that boy will take good care of her.'

Aran still referred to Joss as 'that boy', even though he was now a married man – married to their daughter, if only for a few brief weeks. As he drove on the deserted road north of Heathrow his mind wandered to the day of the wedding. It was just days before the young couple had embarked on their adventure to Casper, Wyoming.

To a new life – a life without himself and Tara.

The wedding ceremony had been a relatively brief event compared with the days-long series of celebrations in a traditional Hindu marriage. For a start there was no elephant – for Joss – and the feasting was confined to a single day - one elaborate day in a large banquet hall in the centre of Leicester.

Formerly it had been a cinema - one of many on the fringes of Leicester before most of them had been converted to Bingo Halls. This particular one had been bought by Aran's brother and converted into a function suite specially for occasions such as this. As many relatives as could make it at such short notice virtually filled the hall, but there was still room to accommodate Joss' smaller collection of friends and relatives.

Overall it was still a joyous occasion.

Joss' parents had met Aran and Tara for the first time a few days prior to the event during which, despite protests from Joss' father, Aran had insisted on covering all costs of the wedding – including overnight hotel rooms for those who had to travel some distance.

Aran and Tara – proving how respectful and sensitive they were to Joss' parent's expectations – ensured they were not *too* over-powered by Hindu tradition and customs. They 'westernised' the event without too much compromise, much to the relief of Joss and Polly.

Once fully airborne and at cruising altitude Polly finally settled and was soon asleep, but waking some four hours later dazed, still clinging to Joss for comfort.

'Where *are* we?'

'We've passed over Greenland heading for the Canadian coast on our way to New York,' he replied.

'New Yor...?' Then she remembered. Her first thoughts were to her parents, missing them already and still not *quite* used to relying on Joss to keep her safe.

'Are you scared?' she asked, reflecting her own insecurities.

'Mmmm... more like excited, I would say.'

He lied. He was uncertain of what *might* lay ahead but was careful not to admit it to Polly. Already he felt, and welcomed, the responsibility he had towards her and to her father, to whom he had vowed, 'I will not let you down, Aran.'

The two Bloody Mary's he'd downed two hours earlier were now giving him a dull headache. He hadn't been able to sleep so he'd accepted the offer of alcohol even though it was, technically, breakfast-time in New York. He asked for aspirin and a glass of vitamin C enriched orange juice to ensure he had a clear head before landing.

'Headache?'

'Yes. It's stuffy in here,' he lied again. She opened the air conditioning and directed the jet towards him.

'Better?'

'Thanks. Yes,' he replied with a loving smile.

He remained looking at her, as if suddenly seeing for the first time how beautiful she was. She nestled into her seat in the recline position, closing her eyes once more – perhaps to dream of home.

Her dream didn't last long.

'Good morning everyone, we are about to arrive at JFK International Airport,' came the captain's voice over the PA system. 'Please remain seated with your seatbelts fastened until we're ready to de-plane. It's a beautiful sunny day in New York City with a temperature of 70 degrees.'

Polly peered out of the window as the aircraft banked over in its approach, marvelling at the sky-scrapers she had only seen, so far, in magazines and Hollywood films.

'No turning back,' she whispered to Joss, with only a hint of nervousness. He held her hand once more – for her sake.

Or so he told himself.

The process of disembarking, collecting luggage, and going through customs took the best part of an hour, but there was no rush. Their connecting flight from New York to Denver was not until mid-day – another two hours – time enough for them to check in before savouring their first taste of American cuisine – the world-famous hamburger and fries. And time for them to relax, soaking up the atmosphere of the busy terminal, people-watching prior to the next five hour flight.

'Wow, this Budweiser is *so cold*,' said Joss as he took his first taste of American beer. It was mid-morning locally but, to Joss and Polly it felt like afternoon.

'This is, too,' said Polly.

Hers was a Dr Pepper.

They tucked into their late breakfast then took a tour of the concession stands in the retail area, comparing choice and prices with what they were used to in England.

'It's not that everything looks so different,' said Joss as they sat down for another coffee. 'The *smells* are different - not unpleasant - just different.' They relaxed for a while, enjoying the new smells (!) with no luggage to look after. It was being transferred automatically and nothing to worry about. The only question mark was against the new life awaiting them.

Time passed quickly.

Before they realised they were boarding the United Airlines flight to Denver, Colorado – the 'mile high city'. They would arrive just after 5 o'clock, New York time – or 3 o'clock in Denver. From there they would take the five hour bus to Casper, whch they decided to delay until the next morning.

The hotel was near the airport in Denver. They missed out on touring the town but they'd had enough excitement for one day. They wanted to be fresh on arrival at Casper and their new employers. The terminal was close to the airport, enabling them to take a late breakfast and still catch a morning bus to Casper with a pit-stop half way in Cheyenne.

'Comfort break, folks,' called the bus driver. 'Be back in 15  or we leave without you.' He sounded as if he meant it but, even so, he still counted the passengers off and then on again before they set out on the second half of the journey.

'Wow, are those *real* Indians?' whispered Joss when he and Polly were on their own. He was gesturing towards an old lady in Native American dress walking with what he assumed to be her grandson beside her.

'I hope you're not forgetting who *I* am.' She gave him a playful slap on his shoulder. 'They *are* my ancestors, you know?' He hadn't realised, or so he claimed.

She went on to explain.

'Yes. Thousands of years ago did you realise there was a land bridge between Asia and North America? We migrated across before the two land masses, separated by what is now the Bering Strait, became two unconnected continents.

'Where d'you think I got this sun tan from?'

She was joking about the last part, but Joss was still incredulous about the whole idea. *Was she serious?* Little did he know at the time how serious she was, and how it would affect events in the weeks to come.

'Very funny,' he replied, but the flicker of a frown across her face made him wonder just how serious she really was.


The tall figure striding towards them as they got off the bus at the Casper terminal met them with a question that was easy to answer: 'Polly? Joss? Did you have a safe trip over?'

'Uhhh...yes. But how did you know it was us?'

'Your clothes. They always give you Brits away. We may have to change that, just so you fit into the climate.'

They shook hands. Ben Jones helped them with their suitcases, leading the way to his pick-up. It was easy to spot, with 'Casper Brewing Company' painted on the side. The bench seat took all three of them. Polly sat between Ben and Joss.

Ben reached behind him to a cool-box on the back seat.

'Beer?' he said, handing Joss a can of Malt Liquor, not bothering to wait for an answer.

Then to Polly, 'I have a Lite beer if you prefer?'

'Thanks, but I'm fine,' she said.

There had been little rainfall in preceding months, so the road was dusty and kicked up a cloud behind them. They cruised silently through main street.

Ben opened the conversation.

'Been a drought for six months now. Since January. Bad for the crops and the cattle – but good drinking weather. We *do* need rain, though, otherwise the harvest will fail and the price of barley we need for the brew will be sky high.'

It was as far as the conversation lasted. Polly and Joss were all eyes rather than ears, trying to take in every feature of the first real American town they'd seen. Ten minutes later they were heading into a leafy avenue on the edge of town.

The detached houses on either side of the broad streets each seemed to have a driveway wide enough for four cars and a double garage set back from the generous lawned frontage. Compared to England the area looked affluent, with usually two cars parked outside on the driveway. Plus, each house was individual, varying in the number of floors and gable ends, with mixtures of wood panelling, stone and brick elevations.

'We really appreciate you putting us up. This looks really nice,' said Polly eventually, until then at a loss for something to say. She was so overwhelmed by the surroundings in what, otherwise, she'd expected to be a less wealthy backwoods town.

'Think nothing of it. Kate and I are glad to have you. The house has been too quiet of late. Our boy's across state in Jackson for the rodeo season and, after that he'll be working at one of the ski resorts in Jackson Hole. He won't be back for a while. That assuming he comes back at all!'

They arrived 'home'. Kate came out to meet them.

'This is Joss, and the skinny one's Polly,' declared Ben. Kate greeted them with a polite handshake.

'Dinner won't be for two to three hours but we have rack of lamb – if that doesn't keep your weight up, nothing will.'

Polly accepted the handshake, and the invitation to dinner, but wasn't sure about any need to put on weight.

'Thank you, Mrs Jones,' she replied.

'Kate, please. Call me Kate.'

But Polly couldn't help but notice how Kate's gaze stayed with her. It was a curious kind of look as if taking in her dark skin tone and looking for any signs of...what? It made Polly just a little uneasy and reminded her of the way some white folk in England - Joss' friends and family - had looked her up and down when she was first introduced to them.

'This way.' They followed Kate inside and were hit by the generous size of the lounge, leading into a dining area with a kitchen layout behind a counter. It was Polly's first experience of open plan and left her in awe of such space compared with home. The air conditioning was chilling, but welcome.

Kate ushered them through into a corridor leading off.

'Your room's through here,' she added. By now she seemed more comfortable with Polly.

It wasn't a room – more of a suite. One wall was just a run of built-in cupboards, with storage over the king-size bed and tables either side. In a bay window was a bench with a set of weights for working out.

'The bathroom's through here,' said Kate, again leading the way off the main bedroom area.

'We share the...?'

'No. This is all yours,' Kate assured them. 'It's ensuite.'

Ben Jones reappeared at the door, the top of his head just visible above the door space. Only just.

He was over six foot tall.

'Why don't you guys wash up and rest until dinner. You must've been on the road for over a day now. We'll call you when it's ready in a couple of hours.'

Ben and Kate closed the door behind them. Joss turned his back on the bed and just dropped, flopping onto the soft mattress. 'This is...'

'...pure luxury!' said Polly, finishing his sentence as she joined him. They lay together, side by side not talking, hypnotised by the ceiling fan whirring slowly above them.

A gentle tap on the bedroom door woke them. Much later.

'You guys still alive in there?' Ben's mid-western drawl brought them back to the then-and-there. Polly rose first, opening the door, yawning as she did so, peering out.

'Dinner's in fifteen minutes,' he added.

Fortunately, Joss and Polly were still fully dressed.

'We must have dozed off,' yawned Polly again, apologetically. 'We'll be right out.' The aroma from the rack of lamb reminded her just how hungry she was. She headed to the shower, calling 'Wakey, wakey, sleepy head,' as she did.

Joss lay there for a further five minutes until Polly emerged from the shower, wrapped in a huge towel, drying her hair.

'You'd better take a cold one to wake you up,' she said.

He took that as an instruction.

'Make that a beer and you're on!'

Afterwards, changing into new pairs of jeans and tee shirts they emerged into the dining room refreshed and alert. Joss accepted the bottle of beer handed to him by Ben, first looking for a bottle opener until he realised it was a twist cap, something else that hadn't 'reached' England yet. He took his first draught before remembering to say, 'Thank you'. He'd woken up dehydrated and now marvelled at the fact that his host had read his mind so well.

By the time dinner was served he was ready for a second.

'If you take the early shift tomorrow you can ride with me into the plant,' said Ben as they tucked into the rack of lamb.

'We start at eight so we need to leave about 7.45.'

'Suits me fine.' Joss was used to early starts.

'What about Polly?' he asked.

'You might as well ride along with us on the first day,' Ben said, turning to her. 'Admin doesn't normally open until 9 o'clock, but I can give you the grand tour beforehand until the Office Manager arrives. We can talk about shifts in the Tap Room once you're settled in.'

'That's enough shop talk,' Kate butted in, changing the subject. 'How long have you guys been married?'

Polly took over, describing the marriage ceremony – which was still at the forefront of her mind – explaining how she and Joss worked together on the differences between their religions and backgrounds. She decided to put Kate - and maybe Ben - out of their misery regarding her skin colour and features.

And she left out the part about the elephant.

'So you're Indian?' queried Ben, as a way to be included in the conversation. 'We sure have plenty of your folk around here,' he added.

Kate kicked his shin under the table.

Polly instinctively felt an annoyance at her host's ignorance when it came to race and nationality, but she quickly got over it - remaining silent, searching for the best answer. At that point Joss came to the rescue with the story about Polly's *Asian* Indian ancestors being connected with the modern *American* Indian nations, through migration thousands of years prior. Polly was pleased it was Joss who'd covered that part, doubly pleased that he seemed to understand and accept the origins of her heritage.

Secretly thrilled even more that he'd remembered.

'I'm sure you'll fit in fine,' Kate reassured them. 'Both of you. Some of the people who work for Ben are also in mixed marriages.' Joss and Polly had never thought of it like that.

'Tell it like it is,' thought Polly, but again she didn't rise to Kate's remark. Did the way Kate had brought Polly's skin colour into the conversation suggest it could cause problems with locals and other workers?

Joss - for one - didn't want history repeating itself.

It could have been a tense moment but it passed quickly with Ben breaking the ice by asking Joss what sports he followed. Ben obviously didn't really understanding soccer – he thought it was just a ball game played by girls – so they soon went on the discuss other things to find common ground. That led to Ben and Joss talking about brewing, again, a fitting precursor to Joss starting in the plant the following morning.

Meanwhile, Polly and Kate compared notes on

fashion and different cuisines. By ten o'clock all four were exhausted and agreed that a night's sleep was what they all deserved.

# Chapter Six

Being guests of Ben and Kate paid dividends.

It wasn't that Joss and Polly were *favoured* by their boss in any way, but living under the same roof as one of the owners of the business meant it *implied* an elevated status.

A sort of privilege.

The plant employed almost exclusively locals numbering less than forty on shift-work - with specialists drafted in from outside. On that basis, Joss and Polly were unique, being 'on the shop floor' *and* outsiders, as it were. At the end of the day (actually by the end of the first month!), both had settled in well to their separate roles after the initial honeymoon period, which you could interpret in two ways. In short, they were quickly and easily accepted for what they were - just fellow workers who pulled their weight.

Polly's bar customers responded equally as well to her.

That included Cary Butler.

Wind the clock back just a few short years and Cary had been the town drunk and troublemaker into the bargain. Finally getting married to local vet, May-Belle Carter, cured him of that. Later on he'd become a landowner. A thousand acres bought under The Homestead Act for a dollar an acre.

He was making a go of it.

He had to. Default on the basic conditions - to build a house on the spread within the first year and to 'work the ranch' seriously and he woud have lost a thousand dollars. Actually, May-Belle's thousand dollars. It was *her* trailer home - where they used to live - that she sold to finance it.

So when Cary turned up one weekend and 'hit the bars' it was deja vu for some, and a surprise for others - including Polly. Part of her deal was to include some night shifts in the Tap Room to the brewery within her work rota.

It was Friday night when Cary first showed up.

It was also a time to let off steam for some, especially those who looked forward to a two-day weekend break. Cary was in town with May-Belle, visiting and staying at her mother's place in Casper. Their 'ranch' neighbours, Eric and Maggie, agreed to stay over at Cary's spread to babysit the stock.

So it was a rare treat for Cary.

He was out on his own. May-Belle decided he deserved it. For the first time in two years Cary was out hitting the bars. The juke box in the Tap Room was turned up loud that night, partly to be heard above the loud conversation that usually kicked off about nine o'clock. That, and the raucous behaviour surrounding the pool table, not helped by the ball-on-ball contact, became harder as drink consumption and enthusiasm increased. It was a quarter after when Cary swung into the Tap Room, heading over to the juke box as soon as he arrived to make sure the music never stopped. *His* music.

*Country* music.

A few songs later, just as Tammy Wynette launched into 'Stand By Your Man', Cary noticed Polly for the first time. He'd always been known to recognise a pretty face when he saw one and Polly was certainly no exception to that rule.

She was just back from her half hour break.

Cary was just back from the juke box, back to his bar-stool.

'Now as you're the prettiest gal in the room - *by far* - you just gotta dance with me on this one.' He wasn't exactly slurring, but it was clear this wasn't the first bar Cary had graced his presence with that night. Correction; that day.

Polly refused his outstretched hand, but politely, in order to carry on serving the guy next to Cary at the bar.

'Oh, come on, beautiful,' Cary insisted, 'it's my favourite. I *forbid* you to refuse.'

Cary lunged forward again, vainly trying to catch hold of her hand just as she was using it to pour a beer on tap. He missed - missed her hand anyway - but caught the beer glass so that it fell from Polly's grasp, falling to the floor.

Where it smashed.

Now, as we all know, the sound of glass smashing

always stops the action. Whatever's going on at the time. It's a sound you simply cannot ignore. You fear the worst. This time was no exception. It didn't stop the record Tammy Wynette was singing, but the room itself fell suddenly into a hush as everyone else stopped what they were doing, saying or shouting - to turn towards the direction of the breaking glass.

'Who's dropped a glass?' was in everybody's mind.

All eyes were now on Cary.

Those same eyes then re-focused on the rugged-looking oil worker next to Cary. It was his glass he'd broken.

It wasn't any old glass.

It was the oil worker's glass *that he kept behind the bar* - his special glass given to him for ten years loyal service with the oil company. He wasn't pleased.

The glass that was now no more.

He was also six foot four inches even without Cuban heels.

'What d'you do that for?' he screamed.

At first, Cary - and the rest of the onlookers - thought he was going to cry. If he was he had a funny way of showing it. A fist swung seemingly from nowhere and laid Cary out cold.

Stone cold.

His head hit the floor as he landed. Badly.

Very badly.

A minute - two - then three long minutes later Cary was still unconscious. Now even the Cuban heeled giant was worried.

'Is he dead?'

The room was stunned. Nobody else moved.

Nobody except Polly, who immediately called for an ambulance. She'd noticed the slight trickle of blood escaping from Cary's ear. He seemed to have stopped breathing.

It was a bad sign.

Rather than attend to Cary her next step was to call Ben, really as a way to get a message to Joss that things were not going well that night. Ten minutes later Ben *and* Joss were bursting through the front door of the Tap Room, at precisely the same time that the ambulance arrived.

'Are you OK?' Joss asked the still shocked Polly, placing a comforting arm around her. Ben had gone to the still figure of Cary before making way for the paramedics.

They moved swiftly and methodically, checking his pulse before undergoing a series of tests to establish the level of seriousness of Cary's injury. Confident he could be moved, they loaded him onto a stretcher. The customers in the crowded bar parted like the Red Sea as the lifeless shape was wheeled out to the waiting ambulance. At least he was alive.

Just.

With more sirens blazing the police were next to

arrive, guns drawn instinctively but soon holstered once they saw there was no further threat. They placed the oil man in handcuffs. He gave himself up immediately - a normally gentle giant until you pushed him too far. Pushing people too far was Cary's main fault and, this time, it landed him in trouble.

Serious trouble of the life-threatening kind.

'Have you called his wife?' Ben asked Polly once the police and medics had gone. Onlookers had returned to what they did best - drinking and spitballing.

'She's going straight to the hospital,' Polly assured him. 'I called her as soon as the ambulance arrived.' She'd found Cary's number on an old list of customers who ran a tab.

'Thanks, Polly.' Ben scanned the room to make sure no further trouble was about to kick off. More police had arrived, taking statements to establish what had happened.

'One of the oil workers will tell the family of the guy who was arrested,' he added.

'Buy you a drink, boss?' Joss had already ordered a cold one from Polly, taking a seat at the bar.

Ben joined him.

'Another day at the office,' Ben announced, in an attempt to underplay the situation. 'Exactly what *did* happen, Polly?'

She gave him a full account, stressing - for Joss' sake as much as for Ben's - that Cary was just being playful, that it was a game that had gone wrong.

Horribly wrong.

'Looks like this time Cary got a lot more than he deserved. Well, you know what they say...'

Ben waited for answers, but none came.

'What goes around comes around.'

But tell that to May-Belle, Cary's wife was who sat by his bedside a few hours later, waiting for her husband to regain consciousness.

# Chapter Seven

It was unusual to see North American Indians in the brewery Tap Room but the two that arrived four days later accompanied by a white couple, got Polly's attention.

It was just after opening time - six o'clock - the time when a few regulars called in for an hour or so after work before making their way home to wives, family and a cooked meal. Polly already had a small queue waiting for their well-earned cold one. Four non-regulars stood patiently to be served.

'What can I get you folks?'

The tallest - the American Indian, Red - spoke first.

'Uhhh...give me and Eric a malt...and....uhhh...two glasses of Coke for the girls.' Red turned to 'the girls' as if for approval, adding, 'Make that *diet* Coke.' He was grinning across to see if his joke had registered with them, then back to Polly.

'You're English? You look...'

'Indian?' Polly anticipated.

'Yeh...so you're one of us.'

'I would have been a few thousand years ago, I guess. But I was born and raised in England.'

'So what happened?' For one moment Polly thought he was going to ask 'what went wrong?'

She would have been right.

'Oh, centuries ago my folks took the land bridge

across the Bering Straits between Siberia and Alaska to escape the hordes and eventually settled in Canada.'

She was using his line of enquiry as a means of having a joke at his expense, except that what she was describing was, in reality, perfectly true. The North American Indian *did* come from the Asian Indian bloodlines - originally.

She carried on.

'Eventually the bridge eroded away and we were stuck here. The rest you probably know.'

Red joined in the pretense.

'You got that right. Nothing's changed.'

Realising they were each making fun of the other, they broke into spontaneous laughter. That got the attention of Red's wife - Chumani. She knew Red had a way with women if he wanted to - but he never did. She was certain of that, too. Even so, she didn't want him to know it in case he became complacent.

'What's with you two?' She came over to join the them at the bar. 'Hope you're not trying to steal my husband. If so, I'd better ban him from frequenting this sort of establishment.'

Red moved to one side, letting his wife introduce herself.

'I'm Chumani. What do we call you?'

She stretched out to shake Polly's hand.

Before Polly could answer, and at the very second their hands joined, a shock coursed through their bodies. It was accompanied by something resembling a moving picture before them - seen *or imagined* by them but hidden from Red, Eric, and his wife, Maggie. Chumani and Polly's eyes were instinctively locked for one brief moment, but long enough for a lasting, identical sequence of events to be buried their memories.

What *they* saw, but totally oblivious to all those around them, was the majestic shape of the White Buffalo: the sacred white species and the emblem of Wyoming. It was as rare as it was iconic. Red and Chumani had been instrumental in bringing breeding pairs of White Buffalo to their ranch, The Lazy B, with a program introduced and aimed at continuing the bloodline. Their focus was on preservation.

The White Buffalo - together with the Lakota legend of the White Buffalo Calf Woman - had special significance for Red and Chumani. It was central to how they first met. Chumani had appeared from nowhere when Red had been injured on a hunting trip. She, and the White Buffalo, had seemed to become one, but interchanging. In human form she had dressed Red's wounds; changing back to the sacred animal she had kept a whole pack of wolves at bay overnight, until the following morning. Red was the possessor of an eagle feather which had been instrumental in saving him from a slow death after being savaged by a grizzly. That 'instrument' had been the spirit of Chumani who had come to his aid, delivering him in what seemed a dream as he lay close to death.

Was the connection between Chumani and Polly *right now* to be the precursor to further ventures into the mystical world of this magical, magnificent beast?

Both had shared the same vision.

In it, there was a herd led by two white buffalo - one bull, one cow, with the cow leading them. Chumani recognised the location of the backdrop to the scene playing out in front of her - in front of her *and* Polly. It was a place where the Lakota Sioux held many of their religious ceremonies and prayers, The Devil's Tower, located in northeastern Wyoming. Steeped in legend, it rose above the Belle Fourche River to a height of over eight hundred feet. Polly didn't recognise it. But she did recognise the iconic animal.

Although still in a trance, Polly spoke first.

'Tatanka Ska.'

Red's reaction broke the spell cast over both women. They left the place in the the vision to which both had mysteriously been transported, returning to the reality of the moment - back to the bar at the tap room.

'Tatanka Ska?' he gasped. 'White Buffalo? How did you know that?'

For a brief moment Polly had forgotten where she was, and who she was with until she fixed her attention on Chumani. She knew they'd shared the vision but she had no idea of the meaning of those Lakota words.

'Did you see it too?' she asked Chumani, doubting her own sanity. 'What *was* it? What did it all mean?'

Chumani stepped in at that point. She already knew - at least she could make sense of *some* of what she'd just witnessed. But sharing it with Polly was still unexpected.

She didn't expect to meet a kindred spirit.

'Polly *is* one of us,' she said - as much for Red's benefit, but also so that Polly could make at least *some* sense of what she'd seen; a spiritual journey triggered by their handshake.

Eric and Maggie also drew closer to hear better as Chumani explained all she and Polly had seen at the point their hands had touched and their eyes had locked. Polly joined in, supplementing any detail she felt Chumani might have missed out.

Chumani ended with a clear pronouncement.

'We *have* to go there,' she began. 'Red, the future of our own herd of buffalo - if we are to continue the line - lies in finding the two white buffalo that, right now as we speak, are grazing territory north of here.'

Red took over.

'We'll talk about this later.' He aimed his remark at Chumani. 'Right now we need to get back to why we came here - to find out what really happened to Cary.'

Then to Polly: 'Can you explain how our friend came to be hurt the other evening?'

Polly was well qualified to answer. She confirmed to his satisfaction that it was an accident, but one that turned into a misunderstanding, and finally ending in violence. Red, Chumani, Eric and Maggie appeared to accept Polly's account. It seemed all too familiar in principle, but so much more tragic when it involved one of their own.

Cary was still unconscious but stable, and under observation in hospital until the swelling went down. Only then could they assess any serious damage which, hopefully, would not be permanent or disabling, given that Cary had survived many a bar-room brawl in the past.

Eric and Maggie worked for Red on the Lazy B Dude Ranch but also helped out with the thousand acre spread owned by Cary, with his wife, May-Belle. They agreed to take care of its day-to-day running until Cary recovered - living at the ranch so May-Belle could visit Cary every day, staying over at her mother's in town.

They finished their drinks but, before they left, Chumani came over for a quiet word with Polly.

'What we two saw - today - could I ask that you keep to yourself? If the word gets around there will be some people - the wrong kind - who will go in search of the White Buffalo purely for their hides. They fetch a high price with collectors.'

Polly agreed, but asked if it would be OK to tell Joss, seeing they were not in the habit of keeping secrets from one another.

'But he really must not say anything to anyone else,' said Chumani, 'and I have one other thing to ask of you.

'You must come with us when we go in search of the herd. The spirit of the White Buffalo Calf Woman has clearly spoken to you as certainly as she did to me. Together you and I will be better equipped to find where they're grazing.'

Polly would have questioned why it seemed so necessary were it not that her experience, when she and Chumani first made contact, was still vivid in her memory.

Every last detail.

'Of course,' she replied. Polly was not only clear it was almost a duty she owed Red and Chumani, but she couldn't disguise the tingle of excitement at the prospect of being part of such an unusual and unexpected adventure.

Above all it was the connection she'd made with Chumani - a bond of kin-ship - that unlocked new feelings and a sense that she was embarking on a journey without really understanding why, or where, it would take her. It made sense of the stories handed down to her of the link between the 'modern-day' North American Indian and the Asian Indian roots of her own lineage. They were historical theories that now took on a level of believability, soundness and logic. They underpinned her own very identity.

But how would she explain *that* to Joss?

### Red and Chumani embrace new frontiers

*Those of you who have already enjoyed 'Wild Hearts Roam Free' will know Red and Chumani and how they came together, and their position on The Lazy B ranch.*

*Both recognise and value their Indian heritage but they are progressive and embrace change and how they fit into the 'new Wild West' in Wyoming in the 1960's. By definition they believe in spiritual connection with a world beyond our own, notions integral to all nations and cultures.*

*Here we recognise many parallels between the conventional, western (Christian) world and that of most Native American tribes. The 'all men are brothers' is never more true if we delve deeper into the culture of the Lakota Sioux, for example.*

*In so many ways there are shared values (values nourishing humanity and community spirit), a shared, central divine spirit, as well as - in most instances - similarities in behaviour.*

*For all those reasons, Red and Chumani are good citizens in their own sense, as well as in those treasured by all 'good people' regardless of colour or creed.*

*One key feature within all this is the natural respect for each other, for each others' backgrounds, as well as for those within the wider community within which they live.*

*Who among us cannot learn from those lessons?*

*But, sadly, how many of us bother?*

# Chapter Eight

It was three months before Red and Chumani set about finding the White Buffalo bull and cow. They aimed to bring them down to the Lazy B from the wild herd north of Casper. In the meantime his duties in the 'dude ranch season' took priority.

However, Red had taken occasional trips to where the herd were grazing, just to ensure the sacred animals remained safe and undiscovered by poachers. They would move down instinctively from higher grazing as summer turned to winter, but for now they kept to the same area not far from the location first sighted by Chumani and Polly in their vision.

She had referred to it as The Devil's Tower - the name given to it by the white man, but the Lakota Sioux were not happy with that name. For one thing, it had connotations of evil as depicted in Christian beliefs to which they felt were inappropriate, counter to their adoption of the location as a place for prayer and meditation.

Going forward, Red referred to it as 'Bear Lodge'. For the native tribes, the area - the rock or monument - had more rituals and stories associated with bears in any case. For practical reasons and for general conversation related to the location of the iconic buffalo, it was safer if they called it thus.

Cary Butler was by that time out of hospital and

convalescing at his and May-Belle's ranch, but he could perform no more than light duties. As a result their neighbours, Eric and Maggie, were unable to join Red's 'expedition' in search of 'Takanka Ska', but Polly and Joss could.

So they did, even though neither could ride that well despite taking lessons - western style at the Lazy B - in the few remaining weeks before the expedition. But any tasks on horseback remotely linked to rounding up two buffalo were totally out of the question. Joss' main duties would be as driver of the Jeep Wagoneer, towing the double horse trailer. And chief cook. They would camp out under the stars so that role, too, would be his focus, i.e. making everybody comfortable after a hard day tracking buffalo.

Polly was invited along by Chumani because she saw her as a kindred spirit. Chumani had a unique connection with all wild animals, communicating with them through some sort of telepathy, as well as applying chants and songs using her own native Lakota Sioux language. She would test Polly to see to what extent she also shared some of those gifts. Chumani put great store in the vision they had shared of the existence and  location of the sacred animals. If they had to use powers other than those of sight, sound, and the reading of tracks and signs for finding the herd, then Chumani and Polly, would prove invaluable. Together, they represented a more potent authority to establishing exactly where they were grazing at any one time.

Ben didn't object too much to Joss and Polly taking several days vacation to assist Red and Chumani. The busiest season was coming to an end and, during the months they *had* worked for the brewery - as few as they were - they'd built up trust  with Ben *and* those with whom they worked.

Plus, if Joss couldn't go, as far as *he* was concerned then neither could Polly. Not on her own.

He wouldn't allow it.


The September dawn arrived on the first day for them to set out from the Lazy B, heading first to Gillette, due north. It was the week after Labor Day and the dude ranch season was over. The roads were quiet. The first snows theoretically could hit at any time by the end of the month but forecasts were good; reasonably warm and dry going into early October.

It was perfect for Red and Chumani's purposes.

The buffalo would be heading south, gradually and purely by instinct; away from high ground and for better grasslands. That had another advantage for the party: if they *did* manage to bring back the White Buffalo then the herd would be more receptive to the prospect of  moving south.

It matched their seasonal behaviour.

Red joined Joss in the cab of the one Jeep; Chumani was driving the other four wheel drive and trailer with Polly as passenger. The plan was to camp just outside the town of Hulett, some three hours drive away, at a friend of Red's. He was one with whom he'd made acquaintance on one of his recent scouting missions over the summer. Once there, they expected to be within a day's ride of the herd in any direction, assuming the buffalo had remained close to the monument.

The rancher and his teenage son would join them each day, making a party of six. That arrangement was doubly convenient in that the rancher's wife offered them a cooked supper on the first night - rather than rely on Joss' doubtful as yet untested skills. After that they would be at his mercy.

They'd loaded four quarterhorses in two trailers. Although Polly and Joss would be *capable* of riding them if necessary, they were principally spare mounts for Chumani and Red in case their own were tired after a day's riding.

The next day they set up camp next to the Belle Fourche River for the water supply, fishing for catfish, and because it was within riding distance of the last location the herd had been spotted, albeit weeks previously. They'd risen later than they'd intended - soon after seven o'clock - mainly due to the late night drinking (too much) and swapping stories.

'Was that legend of the White Buffalo Calf Woman actually true, Chumani?' asked Joss over breakfast.

'*I* believe so, as do all Lakota Sioux.' she replied.

'So this beautiful Indian woman really *did* turn into a White Buffalo?'

'That's what they say, Joss. Apparently two Indian braves were out hunting when they came across her, but one tried to take advantage of her - so she turned him into ashes.'

'Take it as a lesson not to mess with an Indian gal, Joss,' she added, ignoring the fact he already had, in a way!

Joss ignored her last remark. 'What about the other one?'

'He got scared for his life, drew his bow and was about to fire but she stopped him; told him not to be afraid. You see, the woman had mystical powers and could see right *into* him; she could see his goodness. She told him to return to his tribe with a prophecy. To help them change. They were suffering from famine and starvation after The Great Flood as well as not following a good life.'

'Hang on,' said Joss. He'd been frying bacon over the fire and only half listening. He put down his spatula. Now his attention was *all* focused on Chumani, moving nearer.

Polly drew close, too. 'You mentioned a flood?'

'That's right, said Chumani. 'The people had fallen into bad ways, thinking about their own selfish needs and wants rather than their neighbour's. As a result they were being punished; left starving. Forsaken by The Great Spirit.'

'That's so weird,' said Polly. 'Joss' own Christian teachings tell of a similar thing, with it raining for forty days and nights and a guy called Noah building a great ship - an ark - where he could house all living animal species.

'It saved them from drowning when the earth flooded.'

'She's right,' added Joss. 'And there was also another time when the people lost their way morally. It happened a couple of times, I think. I do remember that our God, the equivalent to The Great Spirit I guess, handed down ten rules - Ten Commandments - on how to behave and to treat each other properly again; with respect.'

By that time Red had returned from gathering wood for the fire and caught the last part of the story. Sitting down to join the conversation, he said: 'Looks like we all have more in common apart from the colour of our skin.'

He was looking at Joss but, in particular Polly, as he said it. 'Did my wife get to the part where the Indian woman handed over a bundle and taught the tribe seven rituals and prayers to practice and follow?'

'Sounds like the equivalent to our ten commandments.'

'That's right, Joss,' said Chumani, restoring her place as the storyteller. 'They're practices we still believe in and still carry out to this day. The Bear Lodge monument is a special location where the Lakota still hold ceremonies.'

'You mean The Devil's Tower?' Joss asked.

'We don't like that word. That's what *your* people, the whites, call it. They named it for the tourists' benefit to make it sound more mysterious. Supernatural.'

By Red's tone, they could see he was serious. On a lighter note he added. 'However, we *do* have a pipe to smoke during it all. That part's true.'

'What d'you put in the pipe?' asked Joss.

Red laughed softly. 'You need to ask my uncle. Ask him after one of his trips down to Texas.'

Joss and Polly looked puzzled; Chumani explained.

'He means peyote. And other stuff. Stuff that makes him happy. Gives him visions.'

'Of a better life,' broke in Red, still chuckling. Then to Joss, 'Hey, is that breakfast done yet? We need to get going soon.'

Joss returned to his duties still wrapped up in Chumani's tale. She came to the end of the story while Joss returned to his bacon and eggs before they could burn. But he still managed to hear over the sound of frying. Chumani continued.

'The Calf Woman still returns now and then, so they say. She comes in a cloud, descending as a White Buffalo before changing into a woman so she can communicate with whoever she meets. At the end of her visit she turns back into a buffalo and floats off in a cloud.'

'Until the next time,' added Joss.

Chumani nodded in agreement.


Breakfast was simple and easy to prepare. Joss was acting on Red's orders not to try anything fancy, just to make sure they all started the day with a full stomach. His efforts from Day One were well received, as was his coffee. So much so, Red took a flask to enjoy later that morning.

With pots, pans and plates washed and cleared away they broke camp, heading towards the ranch to hook up with the owner and his son. They decided to corral two spare horses there so that both trailers were empty, ready and waiting for two adult buffalo. White buffalo.

Hopefully.

Only one trailer was taken on the first ride out - driven slowly across open grassland by Joss with Polly as passenger. The other four rode ahead on horseback, scanning the horizon for signs of a herd; a dust cloud. However, if they were resting by the river they would need to be closer before they spotted them, unless they picked up a fresh trail.

They decided to follow the river southwards.

There they saw signs where a herd had rested, possibly as recently as the day before. The earth leading to the river was poached and droppings along the bank were numerous.

The grazing had been stripped bare.

'You wait here, Joss, while we take the horses along the river until we can eyeball the herd.' said Red. 'Keep close contact with the two-way radio I gave you.'

'Roger that, Red,' Joss took on a military stance. 'I might do a spot of fishing for tonight's dinner.'

Red nodded in agreement.

'Use some of that chicken liver for bait, Joss,' he added. 'The channel catfish love it - and I love channel catfish!'

With that, he and the other three took off, leaving Polly and Joss to enjoy the rest of the day until called upon.

Their peace lasted just over an hour - and four catfish - later. The crackle of the two-way signalled something had happened up the trail. That 'something' was Red's party catching up with a herd - or 'gang' - of some three thousand head.

'You'd better make your way to us now,' a voice came over the radio. 'Just follow the river and you can't miss us.'

Joss and Polly threw their fishing tackle - and cool-box containing the fish - into the back of the Jeep and headed south, keeping the river in sight.

'We should be there in about twenty minutes,' he told Polly. 'They must be about eight or so miles away.'

The going was fairly flat and even but Joss kept to a sensible twenty miles an hour for most of the way. The last thing he needed was a broken axle out in the middle of nowhere. He slowed down as soon as he saw the magnificent sight of so many wild buffalo seeming to spring out of nowhere - resting in a gully close to a bend in the river. Red wouldn't thank him if he charged headlong into the herd, scattering them to all four winds. He saw the riders, Red in particular, on a knoll surveying the scene as he brought the Jeep to a halt some way off, getting out so that they could walk up to where they were. Red pointed to two of the animals on raised ground opposite, some two hundred yards away. There were two animals on lookout.

*Surveying them.*

Red handed Joss his telescope. He scanned the horizon until he found them. He was speechless, handing Polly the 'scope without a word. *Now* he understood why Red and Chumani were so passionate about the White Buffalo.

'We need to keep those two like that,' explained Red as he retrieved the telescope from Polly. 'Quiet, away from the rest of the herd, but close to each other. See that little fella next to the cow?'

Polly and Joss both nodded.

'She's the key,' he went on. 'If we can get a rope on her then the cow will follow. She's the wise matriarch of the herd, they all follow her lead - all of them, even the bull next to her - so it won't be easy. She won't want to give up the herd.'

'I passed a small ravine about a mile back,' offered Joss, remembering what Red had said about how they needed to come up with a plan to load the animals in the horse trailers. 'If we can get them that far, drive them into the blind gorge, then they'll have nowhere else to go.'

'Good thinkin', young fella,' grinned Red, appreciating the way Joss' mind was working. 'Then all we have to do is coax them into the trailer.'

'Is that all?' said Chumani. She knew that Red was right, but the cow weighed close on a thousand pounds - about the same as the quarterhorses they were riding. The difference was the buffalo weren't domesticated or trailer-friendly.

Her hint of incredulity was not lost on Red but, undaunted, he made his way slowly towards the two - or three with the calf - three White Buffalo. He told Joss to head back with the trailer towards the ravine he'd found.

And wait.

Once back at the ravine Joss and Polly had time to inspect the gorge to establish that it was, in fact, a *blind* gully. That, plus the scattering of trees and shrubs at the mouth, meant that once the animals were inside he could simply close the gap with the back end of the trailer. The hard part would be encouraging the animals up the ramp without breaking free.

'Do you mind if I suggest something?' Chumani asked Red as they drove the animals back to the trailer.

'It's not stopped you yet,' chuckled Red, without taking his eyes off the three wild beasts. 'What is it?'

'Can we put off loading them to the morning?'

Red thought for a moment. 'Why the delay?'

'It'll settle them down. Allow them to get used to us.'

Red pondered for a while longer. Then he worked out what she really meant. 'What you mean is, allow them to get used to *you*. You think you can talk to them?'

'I can try.' Chumani didn't bother looking at Red throughout all this. She would listen to his tone to guage what he really thought. She'd learnt to read that more than his face. But Red did look across to her as he gave his pronouncement.

'Go ahead. You haven't failed me yet.'

That was enough for her, confident she wouldn't let him down. That kind of understanding had got them through many a tough time over their years together.

They spoke no more about it.

# Chapter Nine

Red relayed the plan to the rancher, as well as to Joss and Polly when they arrived back to the ravine.

Joss started to gather branches and shrub ready to construct a make-shift fence across part of the opening to the ravine. It was barely a fifteen foot gap but it opened up wider inside, giving Chumani another idea.

'Why don't we keep the horses in there to keep them company overnight,' she suggested. 'It'll be better all round than having them tied up. We just need to get some water.'

That, too, went down well.

Soon all three buffalo, plus two of the four horses, were safely corralled in the ravine - safe, that is, after Red had checked out the gorge for signs of mountain lion and black, or even grizzly, bears.

Polly volunteered to take over culinary duties from Joss - with Red's favourite channel catfish on the menu. Unknown to any of them, she'd smuggled along some of her Indian spices and curry leaves, just waiting for the chance to try them out on her new American friends. Joss, of course, was well acquainted with what she could cook up at very short notice.

As it turned out, she only had the four of them to feed. The rancher and his boy headed back to their own soft beds at the ranch for the night, leaving the rest of the party to camp under the stars. But it also solved a problem, enabling the rancher to drive the second Jeep and trailer back out the next morning. They speculated that the bull buffalo - at some eighteen hundred pounds - might need to be loaded into the second trailer and not in with his cow and calf.

Red was the first to notice something different about his channel catfish. He sensed the different aroma - or smell as he called it - while it was gently cooking over the open fire.

But he said nothing.

Polly shouldn't have worried. Red was the first to clear his plate, eagerly looking for seconds.

On that count he *was* disappointed.

'Sorry, Red,' Joss apologised as Red handed his plate out for more. 'I gave the rancher a couple of the fish for their supper. I didn't think...'

'Not thinking ahead can be a problem sometimes,' snorted the disgruntled Red. 'Make sure you ask first.'

Joss took the reprimand as a warning but it didn't stop Red reaching into the cool-box, handing him a cold can of malt liquor. For the first time that day they relaxed by the fire, stoking up the flames against the chill air. If they gave it a good base it would provide more heat for longer, with embers keeping enough life in them for the coffee pot as dawn broke.

'I'll go and check on the animals before we turn in,' said Chumani. Joss and Polly laid out their respective bed rolls. As she passed Polly she whispered softly, 'Come with me.'

Joss heard, and was about to follow too but Red interceded. 'Let them go. They need quiet. To be on their own'

Then he remembered what Red had told him earlier about Chumani's gift of communicating with horses, bears, and even wolves. But her special connection was with buffalo - especially the White Buffalo they already had at The Lazy B.

Polly followed Chumani without question but, as soon as they reached the temporary barrier they'd erected across the mouth of the ravine, she realised she already had some idea what was to follow. Chumani called softly to the buffalo. They'd wandered further into the gorge, perhaps for fresher grass. A shuffling of hooves signalled she'd been heard.

The calf was the first to approach the two of them.

Both women bent forward to greet her. Chumani blew softly into the nostrils of the young buffalo, causing it to respond in similar fashion. Snorting gently. It took another step closer to them - nervously stretching out its neck to engage. The adult cow was more cautious. The bull remained right at the back.

Watching.

Polly copied Chumani, drawing the young calf over to her. At that point, Chumani began to hum quietly, singing in her native Lakota voice. It was a sound that seemed like a gentle warm south wind caressing the long grasslands on a summer evening.

After a few verses, Polly joined her in harmony, both women more focused now on the adult cow.

Slowly and still nervously, the cow took small tentative steps towards them, breathing heavily - it's warm breath turning air to steam as it condensed - then allowing Polly's fingers to run back and forth down the her huge forehead. Polly could feel the coarseness of her fur but sensed a serenity of spirit in the beast, belying the true wildness of her nature.

But what of the bull?

Chumani moved over to apply similar tactics on the massive fifteen hundred pound-plus animal. She hoped her own nervousness didn't show. The barricade was made from thin  branches and brush, some five foot high in part, and over two foot deep, but it was a visual rather than an effective physical barrier. One concerted push from the adult bull and the flimsy resistance would fail and the buffalo would be free.

Chumani continued patiently with her sing-song prayer-like encantation, but to no avail. The bull sensed danger. And what was that sound behind her?

It wasn't Polly.

A chill ran through her as her own delicate tones were suddenly joined by a deep, almost gutteral, voice. It wasn't Red, and it certainly wasn't Joss.

But it *was* a man's voice.

She turned round, suddenly face to face with the owner of the voice. He was Native American, probably Sioux.

But who - or more especially what - *was* he?

Polly had also stopped her song now, facing the apparition before them. They felt panic - brought on by surprise and not knowing the nature of the form confronting them. The buffalo had now become calm as if soothed by the new presence as, slowly, the spirit took on flesh and blood. They were all several yards away from the campfire but it's distant flames still served as a back-light to whoever, or whatever, he was. The face was in shadow. They could see he had long hair in braids. That much they *could* tell. But was he friendly? Benign?

Eventually he spoke.

'Don't be afraid, sisters. I come to help, not to harm you.' Referring to them as 'sisters' was a clue that he wasn't white.

'Who are you? Where did you come from?' Chumani, stepped across, protectively, in front of Polly.

'I am from the Little Bighorn Valley. They used to call me White Bull.'

'Used to?' Chumani gasped in disbelief. 'You mean *the* White Bull - nephew to Sitting Bull? and Black Moon?

'But you're...'

'No longer of *your* world,' continued White Bull. 'Or, if I was, I'd be...'

'A hundred and twenty years old.' breathed Chumani.

White Bull chuckled at Chumani's quick calculation. 'I was going to say "delighted at encountering such beautiful young girls on my travels", but you're right. I would be that age had I lived another twenty or so years.'

He moved slowly towards them, the camp fire still behind him but slightly to one side; now they could see his fine features. He looked to be some forty years old, still fit and muscular, and in traditional warrior dress. They stood, mouths agape.

'Can we sit and talk for a while?' He moved to flat rocks  to one side of the ravine opening, sitting on one and beckoning the two women to join him. They complied, now strangely at ease although they kept their eyes on him the whole time.

'I see you're taking away some of our treasures.'

Chumani thought for a moment, then she understood.

'If you mean the White Buffalo, then yes. We have a breeding program to preserve them. We want...'

'*We* want...?' he broke in. 'I see you easily adopt the language of the white man. They are not possessions. Not yours, nor mine. They belong to no one, but instead shared by all.'

'We?...that's my husband and I. He's over by the fire. I can call him over if you...' She realised then that she was 'introducing' Red into the conversation as a precaution. In case things didn't turn out well - or at least better than they'd started. They also had to show they weren't two defenceless women, alone, at the mercy of an Indian warrior.

'Maybe later.' White Bull's tone was reassuring. So much so that they'd totally overlooked that they were talking to... a ghost? He went on: 'First I would like to suggest something to you - if you don't mind - regarding your...possessions.'

They were won over by his politeness and tact.

'Do you have cows? At the ranch? White buffalo cows?'

'Why do you want to know?' asked Chumani.

White Bull hesitated for a while before answering, knowing his next words would meet with resistance.

'I am asking you to leave the adult cow behind with the herd. Just take the bull and calf. She is almost weaned. It is time for her to leave her mother.'

He looked to Chumani for her answer.

'But we need her for the breeding program.'

'The herd needs their wise matriarch more...'

She knew exactly what White Bull meant. A cow in any herd was the leader, not the bull. Just as a dominant mare in a herd of wild mustang is the leader, rather than the stallion. Without their wise matriarch, or until one could be groomed to take over that position by the existing cow, the herd would have no leader to organise them, to help them when challenged by wild predator or weather. Or by the white man.

Most importantly, to take them to fresh grazing.

'And you're confident Red and I stand as good a

chance extending the White Buffalo bloodline by putting the bull to our *existing* cows?'

'Almost,' replied White Bull. 'Although there are no guarantees. Otherwise the White Buffalo would be a common sight. There would be no need to protect them.'

'I will follow your advice,' Chumani said, reaching out to touch the Lakota warrior's shoulder as reassurance.

But her hand met no resistance.

There was nothing solid, her hand passed through the spectre of the man next to her. He was there, but as a vision with no substance. He wasn't made of flesh and blood.

He *was* a ghost.

Ghost or no ghost, he still found the incident amusing, chuckling as he registered the shock and surprise on her face. White Bull looked and sounded like any normal living and breathing person and she'd forgotten that he certainly was not of this world. He was still just a spirit.

But maybe he was lost.

Polly had remained silent during all this time so when she let out a scream it startled not only Chumani, but the phantom Indian warrior. He looked across and saw the reason Polly had split the silence of the night. She stood frozen with fear as she watched the shape sliding along the dry earth towards her.

'Don't move,' cried Chumani as she noticed the shape, too.

However, as is the case on many occasion when we are instructed suddenly to do *one* thing, we do the *opposite*. Polly jumped up quickly, seeking the safety of the other two - safety against the deadly rattlesnake. Sudden movement acts almost as a trigger to venomous reptiles and, true to form, it rose to strike the terrified Polly.

But what followed next was over in a second.

But to Polly and Chumani it felt as if everything was slowed down to slow motion. Out of the corner of her eye she saw White Bull rise too. As he did he reached instinctively for his holstered hunting knife. In one clean movement he sent the knife spinning through the air past them, the feint light from the fire reflecting on the blade. Its keen edge was aimed at the snake just as it was poised to deliver its poisonous venom to the unfortunate Polly. The rattler's head, mouth agape with fangs bared, lunged forward.

But the head was already detached from its body.

Severed, it flopped harmlessly to the dry earth at Polly's feet, it's sightless eyes still piercing the darkness whilst its bloodless body lay twitching for a few final seconds. The rattle too, eventually silent.

Polly was saved.

Chumani gasped as she turned to their saviour, the Lakota warrior, to be presented with yet another shock. He was no longer the forty-something apparition of an Indian warrior. He looked different - alive, made of flesh and bone, but much, much older. She reached forward ready now to touch his shoulder. This time she was able to feel the sinews beneath his tunic, and a feint warmth coming from it. He looked his age.

A hundred and twenty years old!

He spoke with the same gentle, gravel voice, but weaker - not the sound of one of middle years - but as one who was a centenarian, and then some. His eyes, too, had dimmed. Only seconds earlier they were bright - bright and clear enough to land the fatal strike on the now dead rattlesnake.

It was that same instinctive act, the act of drawing his hunting knife to kill the snake, that had broken his thread with the spirit world. He lived again, on this earth, the same earth from which he'd departed - years earlier.

'I must cease my wonderings,' he said with resignation. 'I've had a good life full of adventure, peace and war - including the Battle of the Greasy Grass - or Little Bighorn as the white man calls it.

'I can still see the face of Long Hair in his last moments before meeting the rightful fate that was to become him. Some say they saw *me* kill him, but that was a lie. But I do recall the look of relief tinged with sadness on the face of my uncle, Sitting Bull, the next day after the battle. Sadly, the triumph over the white soldiers that we celebrated was more than overshadowed by the brothers that we lost that day.

'There is no satisfaction in war, no matter who wins. Look what has happened to us all in the end - herded into trucks to be taken to barren lands such as those far away in Florida. Away from open prairie and grasslands where we could hunt with freedom and purpose. Treated worse than the animals we used to rely on for our existence. Even my own uncle ended up murdered by the white eyes, and not in battle.

'*All* at the hand of the whites.'

The very words he spoke, or perhaps the gravity of his account of the historic battle, seemed to tire him. He shivered.

'Come with me near our fire,' said Polly, helping the now old man to his feet, aware of his suffering from the cold - or was it from the emotion, remembering those days?

Chumani walked ahead, taking a spare blanket to wrap round White Bull as she guided him to sit close to the fire, adding more wood which then spat in protest at the heat.

Red - and then Joss - awoke from their half sleep by the  spitting fire... and the sound of a strange voice.

Who could it be, out here in the wild?

'This is White Bull,' whispered Chumani, softly, noting how the old man appeared to be dazed by his surroundings. The warmth of the fire raised his spirits; he acknowledged the two men - also warmly - as they were introduced to him.

'Will you share a pipe with me?' invited Red, reaching for a special mixture with which to fill it, courtesy of his uncle. It was the greatest honour he could bestow on the legend he had, so far, only heard about. His uncle Amitola had brought the pipe, and the mixture, back after one of his expeditions to the south western states. Their guest's eyes lit up in anticipation, familiar as he was with the 'herbal remedies' that could be smoked on special occasions such as meeting new friends.

As Red had explained to Chumani on previous occasions, 'Sharing a pipe binds friendships, honours your enemies and helps conversations along, ensuring the truth comes out.'

The ceremonial pipe - the one that the same uncle had passed on to him from *his* brother - Red's late father - was filled, lit and circulated - starting with White Bull.

The ancient warrior took a long toke, the length of which surprised the rest of them since he seemed to have trouble even taking a breath walking the short distance to the camp-fire. Exhaling deeply and allowing a few moments for the 'substance within' to take effect, White Bull began to relate the first of a number of stories to a captivated audience.

'I won't have much longer on this earth; not now,'

he announced with sadness. 'As soon as I took the action I did - needing to re-take human form to use my hunting knife once again - I realised after it was too late I would shed my phantom form in so doing. Forever.

'But I wouldn't change a thing. I couldn't just sit and watch our sister fall victim of evil. As with most things in life, it's the unexpected, the *re*actions we take without thinking beforehand  that have the most serious consequences.'

White Bull sighed, relieved as much as disappointed at the prospect of his presence (rather that 'life' in the conventional sense) on this earth now being finite again.

He would finally join The Great Spirit in the Happy Place.

He waited while he allowed those sombre thoughts to sink in, but eagerly waiting for his second 'turn' on the pipe before continuing: 'Since my first passing in 1947 I have been wandering constantly - alone - unable to be with my uncles, Sitting Bull or Black Moon, and the rest of my family. I was neither in your world, nor theirs. Now that will change.'

Red was keen to know everything his fellow tribesman had experienced and was willing to talk about. Breaking Native American Indian protocol, one of retaining a respectful silence with new acquaintances, he asked the inevitable.

'I believe you were at The Battle of the Greasy

Grass.'

Their guest was heartened that Red had used the correct Lakota name for the event, but took on a grave demeanour as those fateful hours filled his memories.

'There is so much I could tell you,' he began, 'if only I had time left in this world. Not a day passes when at least one event from the past flashes before me, good or bad; either way I am always left with deep sorrow. Some things I regret ever happening; I mourn for our people with sadness and anger at what has followed and beset my nation. They say we won but they were wrong.

'In the end we lost. Lost our freedom to live as we chose.

'But we never lost our identity and never will, all thanks to the White Buffalo Calf Woman. She showed us the way, and laid down important rules and traditions for us to follow - so we had a chance to survive and flourish in body and spirit.'

He turned to Joss. 'It is much the same as your Christian beliefs; your Commandments. As long as you respect them, all will come good in the end. However, as with all things, some men follow and some men fall by the wayside. It is the same with us.'

'Sitting Bull did come to England,' said Joss, changing the subject slightly.

'Ahhhh... what a folly, appearing in Buffalo Bill's Wild West Show.' White Bull laughed quietly at this reference to his uncle's escapade after the battle. 'But he soon tired of your ways, your culture. He wasn't too impressed by the English either, or so he told me shortly before he died.'

Adding, 'Before he was murdered.'

He grew silent, thoughtful for a while. Polly, seated closest to him, noticed a solitary tear escape his eye, which he wiped away, saying it was smoke from the fire.

'I still miss him.'

White Bull added more tales of the Old West before tiredness overtook them all. He'd become quite animated as a result of whatever Red had put into the ceremonial pipe, but now even he was showing signs that he needed sleep. It was gone midnight and the plan was for them to get an early start the next morning. The rancher and his boy promised to arrive in time for breakfast so Joss knew he had to be ready.

Before they turned in, White Bull repeated his earlier request of Chumani. 'I do hope you will return the wise matriarch to her herd and not deprive them of their leader.'

'I will talk to Red in the morning,' she replied. 'I am sure he will agree.'

'Call it my dying wish,' he added.

It was to be the last time they spoke and also the last to be spoken by White Bull on this earth. His final words were to stay with her and she vowed to honour his wish.

Dawn broke to find Red the first to rise and, with it, responsibility for feeding the fire before waking Joss, who had the task of feeding everyone. All, that is, except White Bull.

He was gone.

He'd disappeared just as mysteriously as he'd appeared. They were to be his final hours.

'He's probably gone to find the perfect place to die,' Red explained. 'With some of our cultures it's customary for the old, once they've served their usefulness to their community, to seek solitude and simply pass peacefully away. Alone. They choose that option rather than stay, to avoid becoming a burden and liability to their sons and daughters. Dependant.'

Polly wanted to look for him but she heeded Chumani's words. Rather than use, and possibly waste, valuable time on a fruitless mission to find White Bull, instead, and for the second occasion, she was tasked to help Joss prepare their meal. This time she set aside extra for the rancher and his son who, she knew, had probably left their ranch before dawn to join them at the camp for daybreak. Hungry.

'We'll pack up and load the bull together with the calf in the larger of the two trailers,' Red declared. 'You and your boy load the cow in the other. She needs to be returned to the herd.'

He was talking to the rancher, having heard what

Chumani had been asked by White Bull - to leave the cow behind.

'I'll sit with the calf,' she said, realising both the calf *and* the cow would resist any attempt to be separated. But her soothing song and secret Lakota prayers lulled the calf into a state of trance-like calm, while the rest distracted the adult cow and managed to coax her into a separate trailer.

'Meet you all back at the ranch,' called the rancher as he started out in search of the herd. Once found, he would unload the cow to enjoy her days in the wild. The four remaining behind loaded the bull with the female calf in the second trailer.

Polly this time, rather than Chumani, provided the spiritual guidance and charm for the animals. She'd learnt similar Lakota prayers from Chumani for soothing both man and beast. On this occasion she connected easily with the bull and lulled him into submission, just as the calf had been mesmerised. He offered little resistance to being loaded - bribed by a bale of sweet-smelling hay and animal feed.

Within an hour they were on their way to Hulett. There they would await the safe return of the rancher and his son, before making their own way home to The Lazy B.

# Chapter Ten

You never knew *when* Amitola would turn up at the ranch. Sometimes he would be gone for a whole year between visits to The Lazy B to see his nephew, Red.

Today was such an occasion, for 'occasion' it was.

He would bring gifts for Red, as well as for Chumani and the children. This time he came with a flute and a whistle made from eagle bones; mocassins (again!) for Chumani; and 'special tobacco' for Red's pipe. (Again!)

What made it so special?

It was a mixture of tobacco enriched with peyote.

Red's uncle's birth name - Amitola - was quite apposite. Translated into English it meant rainbow. The reason it was so appropriate was down to Amitola always being seen as a welcome presence. He brought the best out in people.

It was a knack he seemed to have developed or - as Chumani was most inclined to say - he had cultivated from gifts with which he had been born: gifts not only of spiritual powers but also his ability to see *inside* people. Furthermore it was his pipe, or rather the substance he put in it, that 'helped' him perfect these skills. During those transcendental episodes, some of which lasted days, the margins between hallucinogenic consciousness and all out subconscious dreams became blurred. That is to say blurred in terms of what was true and what was not, although his visions - at the time, at least - embraced total clarity of thought.

That also included clarity of interpretation.

For those reasons alone, Red not only relished his uncle's company, he actively sought it whenever Amitola came to stay. Did Chumani approve of this alliance? Maybe not so much when Red was also noticeably 'absent' from the family home.

But she understood.

She understood that her husband *needed* this special time in the special place wherever Amitola would take them. And she knew he would be safe. Amitola had loved his nephew and nurtured Red at a time when he needed it most; immediately after the death of his brother, Red's father. The owners of The Lazy B had taken Red in and treated him as their own, compensating for the loss of their own son years previously.

Almost.

For Red, Amitola was his real family, his only blood relative. Conversely, Red gave Amitola purpose in life.

He had no-one else.

We rejoin the story now with Amitola at forty years old and still without a wife, even though many had 'tried'. They had tried, unsuccessfully, to tie him down - to give him the purpose he lacked. They would manage to settle him down for a matter of weeks - a few months at most. It was always the same, the same ending, no matter how fierce the flame of desire and belonging had appeared to burn at first.

It was never love, or the Lakota equivalent: spousal duty. They would always awake to find him gone.

But to where? What lured him away?

It's true to say that Native American Indians are, or were, instinctively nomadic - following the seasons alongside their main food source. For Amitola it was not the buffalo that he followed, or the herds of wild mustang. True, the seasons did shape his journeys in terms of his preference for warmer climes, plus the need to replenish supplies for his pipe. Both factors took him as far south as Texas and Arizona.

But the people indigenous to Arizona and the South West were also a draw for him personally, an opportunity to meet and mix with other tribes. He, too, drew knowledge and enjoyment from engaging with the Navajo and the Apache. He relished their stories, many of which were similar to, or offered variations on, his own Lakota Sioux traditions. But that wasn't all. The limestone soils also offered up another ingredient sacred to him and not found elsewhere: peyote.

The two went hand in hand.

It was their second night away from the ranch underneath the stars. Red and Amitola were treading one fine line, that indefinable distinction between truth and unreality. Amitola had come to the last scene of yet another story he'd picked up on his last 'visit' to the south. In typical fashion, his conclusions differed each time he repeated the same story.

Red never picked him up on this.

In any case, having taken the major share of his uncle's pipe, he was finding *any* attempt at speech difficult.

'Got you something, nephew.' said Amitola, reaching into his gunny sack. Out came his gift.

'A whistle?' Red looked puzzled.

'It's for the kids. Made from an eagle bone.'

Red kept silent, waiting for an explanation. Instead, he got a story - but one he hadn't heard before.

His uncle launched into it.

'Did I ever tell you how the eagle came about?'

'Only a couple of times.'

Sarcasm still didn't stop Amitola.

'This old Navajo chief told me about a couple of alien gods who used to terrorise their nation, thousands of years ago.'

'Oh, yeh?' drawled Red, on the verge of passing out.

'That's right. They were called The Tsenahale and there were two of 'em; one male, one female. Big ole bastards that went round eating folk - especially babies. *If you believe that.*

'Anyways, the Navajo were gettin' really sick of

being eaten so they sent out a slayer - a Slayer of Alien Gods. This Slayer guy eventually tracked them down to where they had a nest. Of all places it was on their sacred Shiprock, or Winged Rock in New Mexico. Apparently the rock used to be an actual bird itself, and had carried the Navajo people there on its back, until it turned to rock, of course.'

By now, Red was snoring, but did it deter Amitola? No...

'To cut a long story short and because I know how this fascinates you so much, Red, the giant male bird swoops down on The Slayer, carries him off then, from a great height, drops him. The fall was supposed to kill him but he landed on a softer, animal skin-lined nest. The Slayer is saved by a lucky charm - his self-belief. Thinking The Slayer is dead the male bird flies off leaving him winded but not dead. He lay motionless until the bird was well out of sight.

'The commotion caused by The Slayer, arriving so unexpectedly in their lair, awoke the sleeping chicks of the female bird. They, too, were large for young birds but they still watched in fear as The Slayer gathered his wits and consciousness. When he came round he saw four eyes staring at him; over him.

'"You gonna kill us?' whined the chicks, shrinking back as The Slayer rose to his feet.

'No,' he replied, 'on one condition; you don't go round killing folks like your parents did.

'They agreed, but it didn't matter anyway. He

picked the first chick up, swung it round, and it turned into an eagle. It flew away and became the first eagle on earth. Then he took the next one, swung it round a few times, launched it, and it became the first owl.'

Red stirred as he felt the fire lose its heat, automatically getting up to put more wood on the camp fire. The night air was becoming fresher, making him conscious again of where he was. 'You expect me to believe all that shit? he yawned.

'So you *were* listening?'

'Nah. Heard it all before. Chumani told me - explained it to the kids one day so they could use it at storytime at school.'

'It ain't just no story,' insisted Amitola. 'I have it on...'

'...good authority. Yeh, I know. The Navajo chief told you.'

'He wouldn't lie,' said Amitola.

'So what happened to the big ole birds that kidnapped The Slayer in the first place?'

'Killed. He killed both of 'em with a bolt of lightning.'

'Of course he did. 'bout the only thing he cudda done. Now can we get some sleep?' Red settled back with his blanket shrouding his head to block out the noise, resting against his saddle. The night sky sent shooting stars overhead, oblivious to them both.

Amitola had a restless night.

Withdrawing from the peyote and troubled by dreams of the myths and legends he'd learnt from his last trip south, he drifted in and out of sleep. One dream in particular stayed with him until he rose again at dawn. He reached for the pot of stewed coffee left percolating from the previous night.

It was still warm.

'What kind of face is that so early in the morning? Nothing bad could have happened. Not yet.' Red joined his uncle to pour himself a cup.

'I got another visitation,'explained Amitola.

'Not a big ole angry bird, I hope?'

'Worse.'

'What could be worse?'

'Someone died last night. I saw his widow.'

'Someone you know?'

'No. I haven't met her yet. The widow.'

'The widow?'

'She was cutting her hair. In mourning. Grieving. He must have died suddenly with no warning.'

'He...?'

'Her husband.'

'How d'you know?'

'Like I said. I saw her. Last night.'

'When you were dreaming?'

Red was proving to be hard work.

'Yeh.' Amitola's tone was getting somewhat edgy.

'You believe in those dreams, uncle?'

'When they're like this I do.' Amitola was clearly

serious. Red kept quiet, leaving him space to tell him his dream. 'She was beautiful. Young and beautiful.'

'Everyone's young to you, old-timer.'

As soon as the words left his lips Red regretted it.

'I'm only ten years older than you, you cheeky bastard.'

Red knew he'd struck a nerve. His uncle was right. Amitola was the younger brother of Red's father, who'd been killed in an accident in the local mine when Red was but a boy. Red was now in his late twenties and regarded Amitola more as an older brother. His only real kin. Red stayed silent again.

The silence lasted for the whole of breakfast.


They stayed out for a few more days - wandering the plains and woods hoping to find wild turkey for supper, but settling for pigeon. They amused them-selves as they always had, even trying a spot of fish-ing in the stream swollen from snows melting way up on the mountains. They had little luck. Peyote played its recreational part in the evenings by the campfire and made up for other disappointments. It also helped them sleep, although they were usually tired enough anyway after a day's rambling. Amitola had no more dreams - not of the kind experienced on that first night.

Nevertheless his moods had darkened when activ-ity was low and chances to reflect on his past life were high. Amitola was reflecting on the beautiful young Indian girl in his recent dream, and how he hadn't really told his nephew the full story, in spite of Red's persistent interrogation for detail. Whilst he hadn't actually met the girl in the flesh - that part was true - she had appeared to him before, long ago when he was little more than a boy. It was when he was in another trance-like state, part of the ritual during his initiation into adulthood.

Even back then it was a face he couldn't forget. Amitola was looking for his own answers. Why had the girl reappeared to him yet again, but in totally different circumstances? This time she was grieving. Red left him to his inner thoughts but they took on a significance as soon as they arrived back at the ranch. Both were surprised and intrigued to see a strange car parked outside Red's cabin.

*Who's was it? And why?*

The answer to both those questions shook Amitola to the core as soon as they entered the warmth of the cabin. And for good reason. 'We have a visitor, Red,' explained Chumani, 'and I'm afraid I also have some bad news.'

If the strained look registering on Red's face was one thing, the shock on his uncle's was even greater when 'the visitor' joined them from the kitchen.

'It's you,' Amitola whispered in amazement.

'You *know* her?' said Red.

It was Polly. Red already knew her from that first time they'd all been at the brewhouse where she worked. He remembered how Chumani had reacted so suddenly at the strange connection she and Polly shared. But for Amitola it was different.

It was the beautiful woman he'd seen in his dream just a few nights earlier, and the same as in his trance during his rites of passage years earlier.

'He's dead, isn't he,' he stated simply. 'I'm so sorry.'

'Did you *know* my husband?' Polly wondered how this stranger knew - this stranger to her and, so she supposed, to her husband.

How did he know Joss was dead?

'No. I didn't know him, but I know you.'

Amitola was now staring at Polly, fixing his gaze on her once long black hair, and how it had been cut so raggedly and short that it barely reached her shoulders. She had cropped it savagely without thought or reason, soon after learning her husband had been killed in a tragic accident at the brewery. She didn't even realise she'd done it at the time. Or why. Not until afterwards. In a daze and out of pure grief she'd taken the instinctive measure, in a frenzy, following the tradition of her ancestors, her true ancestors, the Lakota Sioux

She'd cut her hair as part of her grieving.

He turned to Red with a look of sadness. Red then recalled the story his uncle had told him about seeing a beautiful young girl mourning her lost love, in a dream, and how it had affected his mood afterwards.

It now became clear.

'Shall we sit down?' Chumani offered. 'I'll fetch some tea.'

'Something stronger would be nice,' said Red.

'Make that two,' added his uncle. 'You still got that bottle of mezcal I brought back from Mexico?'

She had.

Normally, the drinking of alcohol during a mourning process would be frowned upon for deceased Sioux, but Red and Amitola decided this was an exception.

'He was white, wasn't he?' Amitola's tone was soft. Caring.

'Yes,' Polly answered. 'Why do you ask?'

'Just wondered if you'd considered how we might celebrate his life.' He was doing his best to be diplomatic, sensitive to Polly's fragile state, but he knew practical things had to be addressed. Was he being too direct? So soon? At first she was taken aback by this apparent intrusion into something that was so personal to her. On the other hand, without realising she was alone in a strange country, dealing with such a definitive tragedy - on her own - she subconsciously needed someone to take countrol. To take control of 'things'.

Amitola seemed to be the answer, as his next question proved.

'Where is he now?'

It surprised Polly to hear her late husband to be referred to as if he were still present. Still alive. But she dismissed it. 'He's in town. With the...professionals.'

She couldn't bear to say the word 'undertakers'.

'He should be buried out here,' Amitola announced. 'We should do it properly.'

'Properly...?' Polly was puzzled. Amazed at how this person - a total stranger to her, if not to Red and Chumani - appeared to be not only taking control, but taking key decisions for her. Without asking. Amitola knew he had to explain.

'You're one of us. We do things properly. It should be done our way, immediately - to give his spirit time to complete its journey into the next world.'

Amitola's tone took on authority, more matter of fact than sentimental, but it helped Polly - helped them all - deal with the sadness of the occasion. He carried on:

'We don't do any of that leaving the body in a tree stuff like some Sioux Indians, nor bury him next to his horse like the Navajo.' Then it occurred to him to check: 'He doesn't have a horse, does he?' He was relieved at the answer, no.

He carried on.

'No? Then we bury him tomorrow and light a fire at the head of his grave each day for four days to guide his spirit. He will be going to meet The Great Spirit in a Happy Place and he deserves happiness, even in death.'

Polly's grief softened at these words. She knew he

was right - even without really knowing why - and she was further comforted when Red and Chumani agreed. They passed the rest of the evening with stories about Joss. At the end, Amitola felt that he knew him, at least a little bit. But it was Polly he was most concerned about, feeling a duty to look out for her, a legacy from his recent dreams about her.

Chumani offered to prepare a series of small dishes of food in way of galvanising everyone around the event, as if in some celebration, albeit quiet and respectful of the dead and the grieving. Polly appreciated such detail being taken out of her hands, with Red, Chumani, and now Amitola, compensating for the fact that her own family were understandably absent.

The burial and events that followed were just as Amitola had described. Polly rarely left the graveside for the next few days, often keeping vigil throughout the long nights, supported by Red and Chumani. Those at the brewery with whom she'd made close friends proved to be equally comforting.

Then there was Amitola.

For once, his fondness for peyote was set aside, at least for the time being. He needed a clear head. He felt a responsibility for which he had no explanation, other than he'd witnessed, or predicted, the demise of Joss in his dream.

Even as it happened.

He shared his experience of that night with Polly, when he felt she was strong enough to listen to his account. She was disbelieving at first but accepted it. The more she'd got to know and understand Amitola, the more she came to trust him. She certainly needed something - and someone - close, to connect with. Further support came a few days later with the arrival of hers and Joss' parents from England.

It was a sad reunion. Tragic.

That said, her sudden acceptance of Amitola as her most valued go-to ally made even that otherwise daunting process - the process of dealing with and sharing her own grief with family - easier to deal with. The biggest surprise to both sets of parents was not only Polly's apparent connection and familiarity with those *individuals* she could count as friends, but the way she seemed to be immersed in the whole idea of Wyoming.

Even that 'immersion' was two-fold. Complex.

For the first part, it was almost impossible not to be won over by the sheer beauty of the state. It swept from prairie grasslands and plains towards to equally majestic landscape of Montana to the north. There was an open-ness and stillness that was often mesmerising itself, complemented by open skies and crowned by dramatically spectacular sunsets.

The second was less definable.

You had to feel it rather than touch *or even see* it. Moreover, perhaps you had to share Polly's heritage and deep roots with which she was born, if not raised. They qualified her as fitting more into the very essence of the valleys, hills, mountains and streams than many of those who counted themselves as locals. Americans. Leastways the white residents, even if their ancestry dated back to the pioneers of the mid-1800's or earlier.

'D'you feel it too, Daddy?' she asked her father as they sat on the porch of her cabin, soaking up the last of the daylight and evening sun. He simply nodded in agreement. She was alluding to the closeness she felt to the world around her now, made even more meaningful now that she had Joss united with it in death. But they also felt the presence of ancestors long gone.

They had just returned from laying  Joss to rest. With Red's permission she'd been granted a plot in the Schultz family cemetary. So far it was the final home of the founders of the Lazy B, Jim and Clare, together with an honorary site allotted to Seth. He had been the faithful old retainer and one of the few remaining hands who'd helped Jim and Clare build the ranch from scratch. The Lazy B had been set up under The Homestead Act by the couple soon after the Second World War. America had received them with open arms, in spite of their German ancestry, at a time when it was less fashionable in British government eyes to be from those origins.

Jim and Clare had been pioneers every bit as much as those who first flooded over from Europe a century before. They epitomised the same work ethic, imagination and drive of the Wyoming founding fathers. More than that, much more, they respected those who defined the true origins of the state - the Native American Indians whose roots reached back not just centuries, but millennia. Those were reasons how and why they'd sponsored Red, an orphan Lakota Sioux, and brought him up as if he were their son, some twenty years ago.

Polly's mother was taking a late afternoon nap after such a tiring and emotionally-charged day. They let her sleep.

'It feels like home, even more like home than England,' she added, followed by an apology. 'I'm sorry. It's not that I don't miss you and Mamma but, for some reason, I never felt as at home in Leicester as I have done here.'

'You must have felt it more than Joss,' he replied, 'even though, strangely enough, it was he who brought you here.'

'It was as if someone else was guiding his hand, I guess, Daddy. I felt that spiritual pull even before we left home.'

Aran Patel paused to think before declaring what he really wanted to say to his daughter. He waited until a flock of Canada geese passed overhead, southwards on their migratory journey, honking almost as a 'goodbye' to them, before he did finally open up to her. Wyoming had touched him, also.

'We feel it too, your Mamma and I. Especially when we're in the company of Red and his wife, Chumani.'

'And Amitola?' she added, but as a question.

'Especially Amitola,' he said. 'In our culture back home...'

'It's the same culture, Daddy,' she urged. 'It's *our* culture. That's the special feeling you're getting. True belonging.'

Polly was excited at her father's realisation of his roots.

'What I was going to say was, before you interrupted...'

'Sorry, Daddy.'

Aran continued. 'Back home in India he, Amitola, would have been a true Patel, more than a headman, but a holy man. I sense a deep understanding and spirituality about him.'

'I feel it too, Daddy,' she replied. 'It's because of people like him that it feels so right being here, even though I hadn't even met him until a few days ago. Already it's made losing Joss just a little more bearable.'

At that point she fell silent apart from letting a steady stream of tears fall as memories returned, as they so often did, of the happy times she and Joss had shared since they'd first met. They'd been heightened even further during their brief times together under the Wyoming sky. Aran placed a comforting arm around his daughter, releasing her only when Tara, who'd been listening secretly by the screen door, came to take over. She was aware of the rawness of emotion that Polly had to cope with, pulling her daughter even tighter into her chest.

'We know you want to stay here, with Joss,' she began, 'but always know that there is a home with us if, and when, you feel ready.'

Right there and then, Polly felt that time would be never.

### Lakota Sioux customs, heritage and the modern world

*Amitola was a free spirit in the 1960s, in common with most at the time who were after the war years, but the roots of his spirituality reached far deeper. They were more profound than the newly-invented and recently recycled search for a greater truth extolled by the bohemian beatniks of the 1950s and the later hippy generation.*

*And there was a big difference.*

*Whereas hippies were diametrically opposed to the values and social mores of their parents and grandparents, Native American Indians such as Amitola, Chumani and Red seated their approach to life through ways chosen to perpetuate the codes and heritage of their forefathers.*

*Even so, that didn't mean there weren't similarities*

*and an overlap in certain practices - notably the use of substances necessary or prefered for reaching those sought-after states where a higher level of consciousness could be enjoyed.*

*Hence the term 'highs'.*

*And, in that, there may also lie another key difference.*

*In many cases within the hippy culture, those methods were part and parcel of the whole recreational package - 'the fun part'; but for many Indian tribes, the use of peyote and its equivalents was a means of attaining insight into the meaning of life as set out by The Great Spirit.*

*Furthermore, the young Native American still relied on their elders for the interpretation of thoughts emanating from these virtual journeys into the unknown.*

*And then there is folklore.*

*All countries and nations have their own versions of very similar myths, legends and beliefs. Those introduced into this fictional account have been adapted from and adopted partly to remind us of how close we all are in some ways. But they also to help us to understand that perceived differences, once examined, leave us not so far apart from each other as we may initially have thought.*

*What doesn't divide us brings us closer together.*

# Chapter Eleven

For Joss' parents it was perhaps harder to leave their son alone in a strange land as they boarded the plane in Denver for the return flight home. Aran and Tara travelled with them, a blessing in itself. It allowed Joss' father to explain how things were for Polly; and how things had changed.

'Polly has found a new home, George' Aran began telling Joss' father, 'and she wants your son to share it with her...'

'even if he can't,' added George.

'Yes. Even if he can't...not in the way he deserved to.' Aran was finding the conversation difficult, but he felt he owed it to George to at least try to explain why Joss was not laid to rest in England. 'Polly still needs him...needs Joss close. But she also needs Wyoming and the memories they shared together in Casper when he was alive.'

'I'm glad he won't be totally alone where he's ended up,' said George in a matter of fact way that surprised Aran.

'You knew old man Schultz, then?' Aran asked.

The owner of The Lazy B had once lived in the same village as George and the family. He'd even worked on a tomato farm until after the war, at which point he'd left to make a new start in Wyoming. Jim and Clare Schultz had also suffered a family tragedy, losing a boy fighting in the Spanish Civil War.

'Yes,' replied George. 'I worked *for* him, actually. Nice fellow, even though he *was* German, even though I didn't really think about it at the time. It was nice of that Indian chap - Red - to allow Joss to be buried next to Jim and Clare.'

Aran agreed. 'It's a lovely spot, looking out over the pasture with a herd of buffalo grazing.'

The journey home was part of the healing process for all of them, with Aran and Tara sat together with George and Sarah, sharing stories of each of their children. It allowed them to  forget for just a moment the future that lay ahead without one of them. Joss. It was also a time for the two families to truly become friends, with promises to continue the friendship, if only to keep alive the memory the joy Joss gave them.

Years later, they'd still kept that promise.


Chumani made more excuses for trips to Casper which Red noticed, but he didn't comment. He knew the reason why, of course, and couldn't ignore it, no more than he could ignore the strengthening friendship between his wife and Polly. They were like sisters - forming a relationship that, whilst it couldn't compensate Polly for losing Joss, gave her a new focus.

Chumani's visits were what they both looked forward to.

Polly had resumed duties at the brewery, shaking

off the fact that her workplace was a constant reminder of where Joss had died in a freak accident. Facing up to that fact, in itself, made her strong. Having
Chumani as a friend also gave her reason to visit the
ranch, and the grave where Joss lay.

'Are you OK working here at the brewery?' asked
Chumani on one late October visit. 'Once the winter
snows really set in, it will be harder for you to come
see me at The Lazy B?'

'Ben and his family have been really good to me,
since...'

Polly was referring to the owner of the brewery
and his wife. Even with Joss gone, they stuck to their
promise to give her a home until she felt the need to
move on.

'I hear their son, the rodeo guy, is coming back for
a while. Is that right?' Chumani always knew what
was going on.

'That's right, but just for a couple of weeks, then
he heads off to the ski resort for the winter.' Polly was
happy with the arrangement, but the brief return of
the owner's son was a reminder that she was a guest
in someone else's family home.

'Maybe I can get you to come out with us,' Chumani said.

Polly waited for an explanation, but it didn't come.
Not straight away. 'How would that work?'

It was the opening Chumani needed to come up
with her plan. 'Give this place until Christmas -

they'll need you here until then leading up to the busy time - but it gets much quieter in January and February.'

'So...?' Polly was puzzled.

'So you can come to live with us, helping us prepare for the new season...what d'you say?'

Polly thought for a while. It was an idea that had never crossed her mind but, the more she thought about it, the more it made sense. Even so, she still had doubts.

'I'm not sure...they've been really good to me here, with the job I like, a nice place to stay...but then again...'

'Think about it, Polly. I'll run it past Red and see you next week. We'll talk then.'

With that, Chumani left.

Polly ran the idea over and over in her mind for the rest of the day, and for the rest of the week until Chumani called in to see her at the bar seven days later, as promised.

She came straight to the point.

'Well? What do you say?'

'It's a great idea,' Polly said, but hesitatingly. 'You know I love you guys, like family. But for one thing...'

'What?' Chumani wanted answers.

'I'm pregnant.'

Chumani was shocked. It was the last thing on her mind, given that it was now nearly three months since

Joss had died. She hadn't even noticed any real change in Polly, and there were no visible signs, no obvious signs of putting on weight.

'How long...?

'I'm nearly four months. I saw the doctor yesterday, and he says I should be due in March.'

Chumani thought for a while, but had already made up her mind.

'I've decided. You're definitely coming out with us, as soon as they'll let you go here. You need family around for this, and we're your new family. No arguments.'

'Where will I stay? You've got a full house.'

'Red and I are moving,' said Chumani. Polly's face dropped. 'No, don't worry. We're moving, yes, but only up to the big house. It's been empty since Jim and Clare, died - and we've had to wait for all the legal estate stuff to be settled. But now it's ours. You can have our old house.'

'Are you serious?' Polly couldn't believe the kindness on the part of Chumani, just when she needed it. 'What about Red?' Polly could see Chumani was making it up as she went along. Had she even had time to talk this over with Red?

Was it ever on Chumani's mind to discuss it with him?

Her reply suggested not. 'Don't you worry about him. I told him that's what I was thinking before I set out today. He's had all day to think about it. He'll agree, believe me.'

It looked as though Polly had no choice.

She worked at the brewery, mainly in the bar, until after Christmas. By that time she was showing, and six months into her term, she moved to The Lazy B and into her friends' cabin in the New Year. Chumani had got it all worked out. Polly was to take over her main duties in administration at the ranch, the dude ranch part, planning bookings for the new season.

'You can work in my office, Polly, but when it gets nearer your time we can set up a desk for you at home, at the cabin. By spring you won't want to be moving around too much and you'll feel tired. An office at home will mean you can take a nap when you want to and, mark my words, towards the end you *will* want to.'

Chumani was right, as usual.

At first, Polly found the cabin just a little too big for one person. After all it was a family home but Chumani assured her that the presence of a new-born baby would soon fill it. In the meantime, as the time before the birth of her baby became more imminent, her parents returned to the ranch to be by her side to witness the happy event. The ranch was fairly remote from the nearest hospital so having them near - especially with her father being a doctor - she felt a lot less apprehensive not having to face having her first baby delivery on her own.

It was just as well.

With snow falls throughout March predicted to be heavy, emergency mid-wife support was left to chance, so Aran and Tara were put to task as soon as Polly's waters broke in the late hours of March 17. By 3pm the following morning, proud grandparents were celebrating the birth of a seven pound baby.

'He has Joss' eyes.' remarked Tara as she held him for the first time. Aran agreed. 'And his spirit,' he added.

Chumani was listening to all this as she was making Polly comfortable, preparing her for a well-earned rest from more than six hours in labour.

'We should call him Wanagi,' Chumani said.

'Translated, it means spirit - spirit of the departed.'

'Perfect,' yawned Polly as she looked across to the sleeping gift left  by the departed Joss. 'Wanagi. Just perfect.'

At ease, she closed her eyes and slept for three hours straight.


Her next visitors were Joss' parents. Their flight had been delayed by the forecast of heavy snows between Denver and Casper, so it was two weeks before they saw their grandson.

Aran explained everything to them when they finally did arrive - especially about Polly's decision to remain in Wyoming for the foreseeable future, to raise her child there, and about the name chosen for their grandson. To say they understood would have been overstatement, but they accepted it - just as they had so readily received Polly as their daughter-in-law.

'At least we have our holidays sorted out for the next five years at least,' joked George to Aran as they sat on the front porch overlooking the ranch. 'Sarah's seen to that.'

It was another promise made, and kept, with the four of them, both Joss' and Polly's parents making the trip together whenever they could each year.

For Polly, her life was about to take a new course with her new friends, Red and Chumani, making sure she had all the support she could possibly want, given that she was now, otherwise, alone with a young baby to raise.

It suited her to being able to 'work from home', to have the office phone line transferable to her cabin should she need to, and to look after Wanagi. If she ever did need to attend to matters outside her office or beyond the confines of the ranch, then Chumani was only too pleased to babysit.

They had become firm friends, sharing the same spirituality thanks to their ancestral heritage, with a growing understanding of each other that enriched Chumani's life as much as it did for Polly. Still, even as the winter months turned into spring with promise of new life, the emptiness left inside her following the death of Joss showed no sign of relenting.

# Chapter Twelve

Amitola waited for the winds of summer to blow softer and warmer before he returned from his annual adventure south of the border, the border between Texas and Mexico.

Historically, for the Native American Indians of the south western states, that border held little significance or physical barrier. By definition they were nomadic, so that sense of wandering and seeking food and home comforts wherever their primary source took them meant, apart from those who accepted the so-called protection of the reservation, they were free.

Thanks to the bohemian liberalisation of certain sections of white man's society during the 1960's, with the growth of small hippy communities, more opportunities opened up for Amitola to cultivate his spirituality. It also provided more sources for the mind-expanding medicines that furthered his search for deeper spiritual enlightenment.

He remained high during most of the winter.

But with the change of the seasons came a change of mood for Amitola, combined with an undefinable attraction to head back north, to what family remained. This year, that draw was stronger. Much stronger.

But he couldn't explain why.

It was not for the want of trying. He was a thinker and usually acted with reason and purpose, planning his next moves with at least some aims in sight, but this time he found himself behaving instinctively. He was also a merchant, a trader by nature, which led him to be worker of people - swapping whatever they had and didn't want, with whatever he didn't have, but wanted. Sharing was also part of the process.

Sharing a pipe was definitely a big part of that, too.

That led to long sessions where he, and whoever he happened to be with at the time with similar leanings, gave way to his emotions and inner self. During these 'excursions' the difference between what was real and what was imaginary became indistinct. But there was one recurring vision that he couldn't shake off.

It involved a bear - a mighty 900 pound grizzly!

For all Native American tribes, the grizzly holds special significance, possessing powers likened to those among man who have the gifts of greater wisdom, leadership and healing. Some say the bear acts as a guardian. For those reasons, Amitola was not so much troubled by the recurring dreams, but intrigued.

What was their message?

He experienced the visions at night, very often after a satisfying pipe. They featured a theme so often spoken about by his Lakota brethren around campfires, the notion of bear and man being interchangeable. Was there truth in it? His dreams seemed to support the myth and became so vivid as to remain with him throughout the day. And it threw up questions. Fears, even. Would *he* wake up one morning to find himself covered in fur and with the muzzle of a grizzly? So far the answer was no, although on some occasions after withdrawl from a night smoking, it felt like it.

Then there was its face.

During such metamorphoses the human face the bear took on was one he didn't recognise. That in itself was unusual. In so many 'normal' dreams we invariably involve people we actual recall from our present or past experiences, but this time he drew a blank. And it was always the *same* face.

But whose?

That would only become clear once he'd returned to The Lazy B the following summer.


Each time he arrived at the ranch he would seek out Red and Chumani first - for accomodation and, of course, a decent meal. There was usually a spare cabin or room not taken up by vacationers on the dude ranch; failing that he would have to camp outside. He'd had a whole winter of that during his excursion down south, so white man's home comforts were his major preference that day. For another thing he was hungry when he knocked on the door to Red's cabin.

He was surprised when Polly opened it.

'Are they home?' Amitola was used to being direct

so there was no 'how are you, Polly'. It was just his way.

Polly decided to be equally brusque. 'I live here now.'

If he expected more information, such as '...and they're up at the house now and I have a baby so *I'm* living here,' then he was disappointed. He had to try harder.

A baby's cry got his attention.

'Has Chumani had another baby?'

'No. *I* have,' she replied. 'It's our... my... first.'

'Your husband's?'

'Of course.' Polly's tone betrayed the fact she thought his question offensive. It didn't help as Amitola remained silent while he seemed to be counting the months since the funeral. He decided an apology was the best way to get this exchange on a more friendly footing.

'I'm sorry. I've been away so long, I lose track of time.'

'Would you like to come in?' Her invitation was another hint, one that suggested he'd made amends for the bad start. She showed him into the kitchen where he was glad to see a pot of coffee percolating.

She noticed him glance across at it, and the fresh scones.

'Would you like a cup? It's fresh.' She poured a cup for both of them without waiting for a reply, before disappearing into the bedroom-turned-nursery to collect the crying baby.

'It must be comforting to have a constant reminder of him.' He was referring to Joss, mindful that it was less than a year since he met with his accident. Joss' demise - the detail surrounding it - had been shrouded in mystery immediately after. Before he could stop himself he asked the inevitable.

'Did they say how he died? If I recall I'd left for the south before the inquest.'

'It was a bear.'

Amitola knew that grizzlies would attack humans if cornered or threatened, or protecting young. But it was still a rare event to be *mauled* by a grizzly, especially in town.

'So a bear attacked him?'

'No. Joss was shot.'

'Shot? Who...?

'Ben shot him.'

'Ben...?'

'Ben, the *owner* of the brewery.'

Amitola was confused. 'Hang on. You said a bear was involved....?' He paused, letting Polly tell her story. It was all new to him. All he knew of Joss' death immediately after was that it was the result of a freak accident. None of the detail had been talked about openly. As was the custom within the Lakota Sioux, it was considered only polite to be patient and wait to be included in disclosure of such intimate, personal events, and equally impolite to ask unless you knew the person well.

His time to be included as a friend seemed to be now, and she seemed to *want* to unburden herself - to him.

'It all started when I was taking out empty bottles to the recycling, in the yard behind the Tap Room. What I *didn't* see at first was this guy following me out. He'd been getting fresh in the bar. You know the kind of thing - sleazy remarks - but I made it clear that I wasn't interested.

'That obviously hadn't worked because the next thing I felt was someone grabbing me from behind, and in a place I wouldn't stand for from anyone - anyone except Joss.

'It was the same guy. I yelled for help, struggled and, the next thing I knew this bear appeared from nowhere, swatting the guy away from me with a sweep of his paw and knocking him clean across the yard. He lay still, unconscious, but still alive. In the commotion I, too, was pushed to the ground. I was face down when the shot rang out. That was followed by the sound of a body crashing down next to me. The ground shook. I raised my head, expecting to see a bear.

'But there he was...'

The words caught in her throat.

'There was who...?' Amitola half guessed her answer.

'Joss.'

Now Polly's body was shaking, sobbing as the reality of what had happened nearly a year ago became as fresh as yesterday. Amitola moved over to put a comforting arm round her. They stayed together like that for several minutes. The very effort of crying so uncontrollably had led to her drift into a daze. He carried her to the couch where he covered her with a blanket to allow her to sleep. He sat at the table. Pondering.

He was trying to make sense of what he'd just heard.

Amitola knew that grizzlies would attack humans if cornered or threatened, or if protecting young. But it was still a rare event to be *mauled* by a grizzly, especially in town. He went over the events in his head while Polly slept on.

What had she *not* told him?

He began to speculate. Filling in the gaps.

Joss could have been hidden *behind* the bear, out of Ben's sightline so he didn't know Joss was there. Just as he was taking a shot - at the bear - perhaps it moved, but Joss didn't. Joss went down but...what happened to the bear? Did it just disappear? She hadn't said.

It was his first question when she awoke, an hour later. Opening her eyes, she was disorientated until she realised why Amitola was there. Then she remembered the baby and went into the nursery to check on him. He was still fast asleep.

'More coffee?' she asked as she returned to the kitchen. He offered his cup for the refill. Amitola was still puzzled but he didn't press her again straight away.

He needed more tact; she needed more time.

'It must have been so hard.'

She answered calmly. 'I don't blame Ben. It was an accident. A freak accident like they always said, but we weren't supposed to talk about it until after the inquest.'

'And the bear...?' he asked gently.

She knew what he meant.

'Gone,' was all she said.

Having to explain it all again so long after the actual tragedy had made her raw with emotion. He didn't press her more. He looked away, feeling guilty at making her relive it all, but he was still curious about the bear's part in it.

What had become of the bear?

He was still thinking about it, taking the liberty to roll one of his specials as he did so, when his eyes were drawn to the framed photograph of a couple on the wall over the fireplace. He moved closer. One figure was Polly, but he hadn't met or seen Joss before so, at first, he couldn't believe what he saw.

'That's Joss? Next to you?'

It was a senseless question.

'Yes. Taken just after we married.'

All he was now focused on was the image of her

dead husband, familiar to him even though he'd never met him.

But he'd seen him since.

Joss was the face of the one he'd seen so many times *in his dreams*, in his visions of the bear transforming itself into a human and then back again. Transforming into Joss. So what kind of a person *was* Joss? Was he living proof that the legends surrounding the bear and man were real? If so, why had Polly never witnessed his transformation before?

Or had she, but never told anyone?

He would have to be careful with his next question.

'Was Joss a spiritual person?'

It seemed an unusual comment but she answered anyway, with a nervous laugh.

'No. Not really. Why do you ask?'

Should he tell her about his dreams, and how they played out with the face of Joss in them? Or should he lie? Come up with a convenient story? He didn't have time to think.

He replied without hesitation.

'I've seen him before.'

'Oh,' she said. 'You mean when you were here last summer? You'd seen him at the ranch when we used to ride out? *Before* he was killed?'

'No. Since then. *After* he was killed.'

His response shook her. Frightened her. She reacted immediately. Decisively. Defensively.

'I think you should leave.'

She backed away from him as she said it but he stayed put. He had to explain himself no matter how implausible he might sound, no matter how hard it might be for her to hear it. But where... *how* should he begin? He elected for an apology.

His second of the day.

'I'm sorry, Polly. I know how difficult this must be, but I have to tell you what I saw.'

'What you *saw?* Saw where? When? You're lying. Why are you saying all this. Are you trying to hurt me?'

She was on edge.

'I saw him in my visions.'

'Oh, right,' she gave out another nervous laugh. 'Chumani warned me about your visions, the ones during your joint - and I use that term under advisement - during your joint *pipe smoking sessions* with Red. Around the campfire.'

She was making a case to prove she knew what she was talking about, making it clear she was wise to his antics.

But Amitola had gone too far to stop now.

'I know how it must sound, but at least let me tell you the full story. At least give me *that* chance and, if you still think I'm crazy, making it all up, *then* I'll leave.'

She gave in. She was calmer now and agreed.

'Go on, then.'

He took a deep draw on his cigarette, then began.

'This happened over several days, or rather nights. I've always had sleep disturbed by dreams and, before you say it, the peyote has helped me get through it. I sleep better.'

She took a sip of her coffee; a signal for him to continue.

'At first the bear - it was no more than a cub - was wandering free in the woods in The Bighorn Mountains. He would soon be looking for a mate, having been weaned off his mother and turned away by the father. But he was happy enough, spending days foraging for food, berries mainly, and whatever small animal he could catch. He was fast, already able to run up to 30 miles an hour. He never went hungry.

'One day he became caught in a bear trap left out by poachers but, before they came back to check on them, a young Sioux maiden happened along.'

'Who was she?' asked Polly.

'I never saw her face. She was the chief's daughter. Don't ask me how I know. She released him and bathed his wound, making a poultice of herbs and mosses she found in the forest, staying with him and even feeding him until he got better.'

'The bear didn't try to kill her?'

'Why would he? She'd saved his life. They'd hidden away together in a nearby cave so the poachers never found them.'

'So, what happened when he got well again?'

Amitola looked straight at her so she could see what he was about to tell her, as crazy as it might sound, was true.

'Two weeks later the bear could walk without any problem. The wound had healed and no bones were damaged. On the  morning just before he left, she awoke at dawn to see the bear looking at her. He'd lain beside her, studying her in her sleep. She looked deep into his eyes.'

His next words came as no surprise.

'They were full of love.'

'Hey. This is starting to get weird,' she said. 'The bear fell in love *with an Indian girl?*'

'It's not a strange as it seems,' he insisted. 'There are many tales of such things happening, stories from many of our tribes with a heritage of a strong connection with bears. We even learn from them. You know they are said to be able to heal themselves, don't you?'

'But not on this occasion.' She broke into a smile. She was pleased with herself for getting one in, as she called it.

'The bear didn't need to,' said Amitola, remaining serious. 'Anyways, I can only tell you about my dream. I'm telling you how it happened. I'm not making it up.'

'So, what does this have to do with me,' she asked.

'I'm coming to that.'

She kept silent again. Eager for the next stage of

his story.

He continued.

'The maiden saw the love in his eyes as they both lay there for a while, sharing thoughts with an unspoken language as the sun rose to warm their bodies. They could feel the forest starting to come alive, taking it all in, connecting in a way that only man and beast can. It was a spirituality born at a time when The Great Spirit gave birth to us all. Including animals.'

'And especially bears,' added Polly.

'Yes, especially bears,' he agreed, happy that she seemed to see some truth in what he was telling her. 'Eventually the bear rose and, with eyes that said 'Goodbye', he turned to walk slowly away and deep into the forest.'

'It was "Goodbye", but not "Farewell"?' she suggested.

He hesitated. 'How did you guess?'

'It just seemed right. It's a love story after all, isn't it? They always come back, don't they?' She seemed lifted by the tale.

'By 'they' do you mean 'men'?'

'Maybe bears, too.' He was glad her mood had lightened. It showed she believed his story and wanted to hear more.

'You're right again. 'Mato Cikala', or 'Little Bear' did return, but not as a bear.' Amitola used the Lakota name. 'He came back - to her - as a man.'

Her imagination was set alight; running rife. She gasped.

'As a man? You mean as... Joss? That bear *could have been my husband?*'

Amitola didn't answer. He didn't need to. She took over.

'He was always saying he was so sure he'd been on this earth before, but he never said *as a bear!* So he was protecting me. The girl in your dream...*must have been me.*'

'*Could* have been,' he corrected. 'I never saw her face.'

'You would have remembered.' She was teasing him now; perhaps even flirting. But he missed it.

'Does it make it any easier?' he asked.

She pondered for a while, still deep in thought. She disappeared into the next room, re-emerging with her baby son.'

'We called him Wanagi,' she said, placing him on the couch. 'It means...'

'...spirit of the departed. Yes, I know,' he broke in. 'A perfect choice...for a cub.'

The last sentiment was lost on her. He explained later that, if what they both now knew or, at least what they suspected was right, then Wanagi would indeed become a guardian for those around him, and for those whom he would love.

It would be his life's work; his mission.

# Chapter Thirteen

It was to be their secret.

They vowed not to tell a soul to avoid looking ridiculous and eccentric, and so life could go on as normal - normal for Wanagi going forward. They agreed that if they were ever to disclose what they had just shared with each other, with Red and Chumani, then they would consult each other first.

When the coroner's verdict was made public it *did* contain statements that there *had* been a bear, that it *had been* shot and wounded, and then escaped. Joss had been shot, and killed, as he ran out of the brewhouse when he heard Polly scream, shot as he came into the line of fire.

His death was put down as collateral damage; friendly fire.

A tragic accident.

Ben, of course, knew different.

He *had* seen the bear; he *had* shot it; and he had shot - *and killed* - it. There was no doubt in his mind that Joss was nowhere to be seen *at the scene*, or in the vicinity, and there was no bear that had survived and escaped, wounded.

He had *killed* it. He was certain.

He was also certain that he'd seen the impossible; a bear changing into a man. But he couldn't tell a living soul. Not Polly, nor his wife and family, nor even his priest - or coroner.

No. Definitely not the coroner.

In the circumstances, whilst the verdict cited Joss' death lay at the hands of Ben, he wasn't charged with any crime. They believed his version that a bear was discovered in the lot at the rear of The Tap Room - putting it down to scavenging for food, as they sometimes did. Luckily, this part was corroborated by the guy who'd started the whole thing. The drunk.

By attacking Polly.

But that didn't dull Ben's sense of guilt, blaming himself for Joss' death. From that he would never recover. How could he possibly make up for it?

He did find a way.

Ben - and his wife, Kate - were good people. They had taken to both Polly and Joss during the short time they lived with them plus, they were good workers. It came as a surprise, however, when a letter came some weeks after the verdict containing a gift - but no ordinary gift.

It was for Wanagi.

It was a a Trust Fund set up by Ben and financed for Wanagi's University Of Wyoming education in Laramie - at UW, or 'U-dub' as it was affectionately called. Ben was clear that he would also pledge support for any special educational needs that her son might need during primary and High School education, with a separate Foundation.

Ben and Kate knew they couldn't make up for the loss of Wanagi's father. Offering money would be an insult. This gift, or compensation, recognised the damage inflicted by 'the accident' and was seen by them - and, thankfully, Polly, too - as the right and proper gesture to make. Polly graciously accepted the fund for her son. She knew Joss would have approved. But to say that life returned to normal at the ranch would be to ignore the impact that Joss' death had on everyone. That went way beyond the Ben, Sarah, the brewery and the townsfolk he had come to count as friends, and included Red and Chumani.

Plus Amitola, of course. It was he who had solved - if that is the right word - the mystery surrounding Joss' shooting. It made sense, at least for Polly. Did it make it any easier for her? That's hard to say. But it did bring them close. Amitola had shared his insight, giving the tragedy some reason for her. Even some purpose. But where did it leave him?

It left him still wandering, without any real ties apart from those to his nephew. They assumed that was why he decided to stay close that summer - seemingly looking for his own purpose of a different kind. A purpose to his life. Not 'bumming around' as Chumani would put it. But was there something else this particular year that had dampened his enthusiasm for spending days exploring the more remote areas of the country, just to get away from people?

Away from white people, at least.

He even persuaded Red to find him some work at the dude ranch. He had the skills, roping and branding, mending fences, watching over a herd of cattle or buffalo. His own quarterhorse, one that he'd had since it was weaned, was a leading cutting horse in the region. He'd won competitions at local rodeos although he never ventured as far as Jackson Hole for the main circuit, even though some fellow Lakota Sioux were now big names there and making a lot of money.

His reputation for breaking a wild mustang was legendary and a well-kept secret, although Red knew it. He knew all the Indian tricks. Amitola would take off for the the day on his own horse with a couple of mustang on leading rein behind him. They'd be as wild as the day they were born. Later that same evening he'd return riding one of the mustang, no longer 'wild', with his own horse on leading rein together with the other mustang also 'broken'.

'Broken' was probably the wrong word. 'Rideable' they certainly were, even if they weren't fully trained and schooled. He would head for the North Platte River where he would ride into a shallow part and, in turn, ease himself off his own mount and onto the back of the mustang.

First one, then the other.

Not only would the mustangs each be relatively compliant by learning signals from his quarterhorse, but the few feet of water would prevent each mustang from unseating him, purely by allowing water to restrict their movement. He would spend all day if necessary until he sensed it was safe to take the untamed horses for a slow ride across the grasslands, with him in the saddle. At first, he usually rode them up the side of gradually rising high ground but, on the way down and descending, he would switch to his own horse in case the mustang still had thoughts of getting away from him.

Some said he understood animals - and horses in particular - more than he did people. That was only partly true, since he could travel from Wyoming down to Mexico without knowing a soul, and still be sure to find those who would take him in, whether among his own people or other tribes. Or even, if they were white - and friendly - in some barn overnight.

Amitola knew many people although he rarely allowed many of them to get close. That was one reason he was forty years old, give or take (he never really knew) and was still unmarried. That wasn't to say he didn't have women he knew he could go to, but his relationships would barely last the winter.

He now felt the need to change all that.

But why? And for whom? Would that change be a more permanent move for him *this time*?


Since that first conversation with The Author or, at least, the first conversation Joss *could recall - in his second life* and events that took him to Wyoming - he felt himself blessed.

Blessed in two ways.

He felt privileged to be alive for this second time,

or so it would seem. He'd taken The Author's word for that, even though he had no clear image or recollection of what his life had been like *the first time*. Nothing, that is, apart from brief flashes of memory, none of which had made sense.

We all seem to have our own recollections of past memories at some time or other. Sometimes regularly. Those '*I'm sure I've been here before*' events are typical of the ones we experience most, perhaps all of us, albeit rarely. They can occur during our waking hours - for which science, allegedly, has an explanation - so they are apparently normal and logical. However, the cynics amongst us might discount them as just theories that have yet to be disproven. Unsolved mysteries. Unreal.

But most of us just simply accept them.

Joss did a lot of 'accepting' during his waking hours in his second life, and even more in the form of visions. You could say that the past invaded his consciousness at all levels. There was something predatory in their nature, like an unrelenting guilt. But what disturbed him most was the context within which he'd appeared to live in some past life. Most unsettling of all was the form that he apparently took during the fantasies that besieged him *in* his dreams. Those episodes recurred most often and stayed with him. He woke up with them still in his head, thoughts transported from dreams to his waking hours. It was like a separate existence, one where he found himself seeing his former world through the eyes of another.

Not another person, but through those of a bear.

The setting and terrain were indeed different. He was in another country, miles from the familiar countryside of rural Leicestershire. It was a location of an unfamiliar kind - unfamiliar at first. Gradually, however, he became at home in the sweeping grasslands, the rocky terrain, the snow-capped mountains, and the woods thickening into forests. He would ramble for days, lost, not knowing where he was going, but not lost so that he was afraid or uncomfortable with his surroundings.

He felt at home.

He saw, mixed with, and even communicated with other bears too, using signs and movements rather than words. That experience in itself felt familiar, an affinity with other bears stretching as far back as he could remember - leastways in the context of his visions and dreams. Nor could he recall when he actually *knew* he was a bear himself, but he was reminded of it each time he saw his reflection in a river or lake. Until...

Until one day it all changed.

That was the start of a different series of imaginings where, whenever he caught his reflection in a stream, he saw a different image. Not a bear but the image of a man. Initially, a young man, who he came to recognise as himself. In those instances - and in those alone - he would also sense the presence of a another. And there lay the other difference. It wasn't the presence of another bear or animal.

But of a girl.

The two situations and occurrences always went together; that is, her being present, watching; him being himself, *Joss.* She was a beautiful girl with jet black hair and eyes that, although grey, shone with a striking brilliance. They set her whole face alight; alive. She would be about the same age as himself, but the furs and animal skins in which she dressed revealed she was a Native American. Yet, how was he *able* to identify her as such?

How did he know what an Indian looked like?

That could only be rationalised and explained by his ability to draw knowledge and reference from his so-called 'normal', waking existence; from his current 'now' state and able to transfer such references to his spiritual journeys. Call it instinct. This principle was the only explanation for his perception that she was beautiful, even though he wasn't allowed to see her face. So how *did* he know? Instead of actually *seeing* her beauty, the idea that she *was* beautiful was somehow based on his involuntary attraction towards her. feelings based on the fact he was overcome by strong emotions - emotions new to him that he could barely describe, let alone control. They were emotions that he and 'this girl' seemed to share, together with one other fundamental that bound them.

They both drew strength from The Great Spirit.

They accepted and respected this concept as the over-arching Power guiding them, governing their destiny and fortune as they journeyed through life. The Great Spirit was imagined by them as having human form, too, without them knowing why. The same Power remained with him as he reverted back to bear form, but when that happened the image of The Great Spirit ceased to take on any form. Any *human* form.

Even so, he still 'felt it'. Felt the Power over him.

All bears did, displaying it in their rituals and when calling on strengths and knowledge that defined their species. As with other bears, he was infused with that wisdom, the gift of healing, as well as the duty of the guardianship over others.

It was unsurprising, therefore, that his natural sense of guardianship developed to such a high level towards the Indian Girl, that he fell in love with... Canoni. He had given her this name, meaning 'Wanderer in the Woods', because that's where and how he, in human form, first encountered her.

But it remained a secret love, primarily because she knew  he had this alter ego as a bear, potentially leading to a union not only forbidden in her Lakota culture, but one where she would be cast out and shunned by her own people. As much as the Native American people drew so much inspiration from bears, there *were* boundaries. Lines you didn't cross.

All these thoughts and virtual experiences occurred before he was finally destined to see and ultimately get to know Polly, the girl on the L27 Midland Red bus journey each morning to the office where he worked. In what might be considered the real world back in Leicestershire. He never connected the two because... why would he? To make things even more vague, there was the other presence in that life, the ever-presence of The Author, that he neither understood nor welcomed.

All this only made his whole state of mind more confused.

As the nights came and went, Joss' 'dream' story progressed through the various stages of his secret relationship with his Indian Girl lover, until the inevitable happened.

Canoni and Joss' secret was discovered.

One of the young men in her tribe had also grown a strong attachment to Canoni, but all his advances had so far been rebuffed. As a chief's daughter she would have to marry someone whilst she was still young and intact, and she would have to choose a husband from her tribe who displayed all the qualities befitting her status.

This particular young man considered himself the most suited, becoming relentless in his pursuit of her. But it came to a brutal end one night when he followed her as she disappeared into the dark forest to meet her Wicasa-Mato.

Her Man-Bear; Joss.

The young man from the tribe stayed out of sight at first but, as soon as they were both clear of the Indian camp he caught up with her. He demanded to know where she was going, suspecting she was meeting a lover from another tribe without her father's blessing, and to his own great disapproval. Harsh words were spoken and it was soon evident - to anyone who might be watching - that she was in danger of him doing her harm. He was intensely jealous.

There *was* someone watching; Wicasa-Mato.

As Canoni struggled with the young man who'd followed her, Joss - in bear form - acted decisively and instinctively. After all, by nature he was a guardian to those in danger. With lightning speed he emerged from the thicket where he'd been waiting, charging into the clearing with the sole intention of rescuing her.

Seeing the bear almost upon him, the young man drew his hunting knife ready to defend himself - to protect both himself and Canoni, for he had no reason to believe the bear and Canoni had *arranged* a meeting in the forest. The young man lunged with his knife but the bear was too fast. With one swipe of one paw Wicasa-Mato disarmed his adversary then, raising himself to his full height - he was eight feet tall on his hind legs - he batted the young man, catching him at the side of the head with such force that he was killed instantly.

Canoni was in fear of her life too until she saw the

Wicasa-Mato gradually transforming into the handsome young man she was expecting.

Joss.

They embraced, relieved they were both unharmed until they looked down. The young Indian tribesman was lying at their feet, dead. Killed by the bear.

Killed by Joss.

But the worst was yet to come. The Great Spirit was angry that their illicit liaison had resulted in an innocent tribesman's death. Wherever you pointed the blame, a tragedy had happened and retribution of some kind had to follow. Canoni was instructed by The Great Spirit to return to the Indian camp. There, she would explain how she and the tribesman had been gathering firewood when they were set upon by a bear, who killed her young would-be suitor, as perceived in their eyes, before disappearing into the forest.

The Great Spirit then announced his sentence.

'Wicasa-Mito, you have committed a great wrongdoing. You are to live the remainder of time wondering the forest. Keep away from the Indian tribe, and keep away from Canoni.

'You must forget her. Go about your existence totally in bear form, with no transformation to human, and with no engagement with humans until I, The Great Spirit, decide you have been punished enough, and release you.'

Wakan Tanka, The Great Spirit, had spoken.

There was mention earlier in this account of Joss being blessed in two ways; the first being that he felt fortunate to be alive again.

The second was he would at last see the face of Canoni.

As we have now discovered, he met and fell in love with her all over again as Joss, and not as a Wicasa-Mato. Canoni, of course, was Polly. It is like history repeating itself. Joss, or was it Wicasa-Mato? and Polly, or was it Canoni? are ripped apart yet again. Joss' second life comes to an end, finally, but this time by human hand (or gun). Joss is slain in the very act of saving Polly from her fate at the hands of the drunk in the parking lot in The Tap Room.

So what now would lay ahead for Polly?

Would Joss, or his counterpart, Wicasa-Mato, ever return to walk this earth and be part of Polly's life?

Or would that be left to her son - *their* son; Wanagi?

# Chapter Fourteen

Amitola had risen earlier than normal - to feed the horses before making his own breakfast. By the time he'd eaten, checked his backpacks for the journey and, finally, made sure his firearms were in good order, his mounts had finished their oats and nuts and would soon be ready for the off. The last thing he wanted at the beginning of his day's ride was for one of them to go down with colic after a few miles because he hadn't allowed them enough time to digest *their* breakfast.

A twisted gut could be fatal if not treated properly.

'Where d'you think you're going?' The voice came from across the yard. It was Polly.

'Not sure yet. Why d'you ask?'

'I'm coming with you.'

Amitola paused halfway through tightening the cinch on the horse he would be riding; his prize quarterhorse.

'Did you hear me? I said...'

'I *heard* what you said,' he interrupted. 'What makes you think I want company?'

'We all need company. Sometimes,' she said. This time she paused before coming out with what she really meant. 'Maybe *I* need the company.'

Amitola stopped what he was doing altogether to hear what else she had to say. She'd already wrecked his concentration - his focus on the mental list of 'things to do before I leave' he was carrying in his head. Now he had more to think about.

He spoke softly, suppressing his mild irritation.

'I can't take you and your little'un on the trail. It's too risky,' he began. 'And, anyway...'

She didn't let him finish. 'Chumani's looking after Wanagi. I arranged it last night.'

'Last night?'

'Over supper,' she replied. 'That's when she told me about your trip. It was her idea for me to come. She said I might even be useful. Two heads, and all that...'

'That normally applies if there's a problem,' he said.

'Maybe there is?'

'And what might that be?' He was intrigued, sitting down to roll one of his 'specials'. As always, she had to comment.

'A bit early for that stuff, don't you think?'

'That attitude would be among the reasons you *shouldn't* be coming.' He ignored her and carried on rolling, putting the end of the 'cigarette' to his lips and lighting it before explaining further.

'We'll be... correction... *I'll* be gone for several days, riding most of the time, meagre rations, no soft bed, and -'

'No ceiling; just the stars,' she added. 'Sounds like heaven.'

'It's work; not leisure,' he countered. 'I promised

Red I'd bring back a mustang stallion. He needs another youngster to strengthen the line. I saw one just south of the North Platte River a while back. I was going to go look for him.'

She wasn't taking 'no' for an answer. 'Then there *is* no problem. I asked for a few days off,' she said. 'Gimme ten minutes and I'll be back with my gear. Time enough for you to find me a horse, and smoke that...thing.'

Defeated, he did as he was told. By the time she got back he had one of the other fed-and-watered mounts ready for her.

'Hope you've got your own supper,' he said as they set out. 'We'll try and cover as much ground as we can on the first day, then we'll take it easier.'

They rode until reaching a forested area and close to water, where they rested for two hours at high sun. They were deep into the country and away from the main highway. The horses were tethered, but close to them. Whilst attacks from mountain lions, wolves and even grizzlies - on horses - were uncommon, Amitola erred on the cautious. Even so, they felt relaxed, finding time to talk properly. It was their first time alone since he'd turned up at her cabin after a winter wandering the south.

'You still miss him,' he asked, handing her a cup of hot coffee. She wasn't sure if was a question or statement.

'Every time I wake up to Wanagi crying,' she

replied. 'So, yes. I'll never forget Joss.'

'You can't grieve for ever.' He took a sip from his own cup. She wondered why he took such an interest in Joss.

And in her.

'Have you ever had someone? Someone close?'

'A woman, you mean?' She didn't answer, so he continued. 'Stuff got in the way but, yes, there was someone. Just the one, about the time I stopped being a boy and had to go through the ceremony to become a man.'

'How does that work?' she asked, expecting him to cite one of those stupid rituals where the boy is dragged into a night of drunkenness on the town, only to end up in some sleazy brothel and, later, emerging as a man. He assured her that wasn't the case and he was surprised that she really *didn't know* about the true Lakota custom. He decided that misconception had to change. He went on to describe rituals that went back centuries. She now seemed less concerned about his apparent 'first love', if that's what it was and was more intrigued about his rites of passage.

'When we reach sixteen, it's time for all Sioux males to be tested. We have to go off for days, walking into the wilderness without food and water, or even a horse, with just basic tools and clothing to survive. This usually lasts four days and four nights, during which we pray to The Great Spirit to grant us our vision of the path we should take in the future, and how we should conduct our lives. That state can only be reached by fasting, lack of water, and very little to protect us from the cold night air and hot mid-day sun.

'If we survive - and some don't, because there are bears, cougars and wolves out there and we grow too weak to defend ourselves - we head back to camp where we give an account of what we saw to the elders.'

'What you *saw*? You *hallucinate*?' she asked.

'If we're lucky. Chosen. We may lapse into a coma-like state, besieged by strange dream-like episodes even if we appear to be awake. We have to remember them when we retur for the elders - or shaman - to interpret. From them, they are able to map out our life course. Our future.'

'What was yours...?'

'What was my 'what'?' he asked.

'Your vision. Your direction in life. What did the elder say? Did he tell you to go off wandering all over the place for months on end like you do? Is that why you do it?'

She could tell she was touching on a nerve and he wondered who she'd been talking to. He suspected Chumani. He took out his tobacco and started to roll another one of his specials, partly to annoy her, partly to help him concentrate. Events in his boyhood were gradually coming back to him but his pipe - and his 'specials' - always seemed to sharpen his senses.

They sharpened his memory, too. He went on with his story.

'I remember being on the ice. It was cold and we were dressed in furs, a band of perhaps twenty of us including women and children. It's unclear now whether we were fleeing somebody or something; or whether something was trying to kill us. Or maybe we were going where the food was plentiful. Following herds of horses, caribou and bison. All I can really remember is we couldn't go back, and we *had* to go forward towards the rising sun. East.

'After days and days of travelling over the ice - we'd left firm land behind us and somehow knew there was the promise of good land ahead - we saw smoke rising and could smell it on the damp air. We could smell food cooking, too. Fish. It was the smell of fish being cooked in a camp by people just like us. Like us, they were also seeking something. Seeking safety.

'None of the predatory animals bothered us specifically, but they did seem to be following us. We caught glimpses. The bears were white. I remember that bit. They were like brown grizzlies - big when they stood on their hind legs, and fierce - but they were white. So were all the other animals like wolves and foxes, even hare and rabbits. All white.'

'What about buffalo?' she asked.

He knew why she asked that. 'No. They were brown - tan - like they always are. Wood bison, descended from the Steppes. Bigger than the ones we have here, now. But there were no white buffalo, not like the ones Red and Chumani have.'

She decided to switch the conversation.

'They were friendly? These new people?' she asked.

'Yes,' he replied. 'They were like us. Brown-skinned. We could even understand their language. First they offered us food then the next day we travelled together - south.'

Amitola sat silent for a while, tugging on his cigarette, casually staring into the distance. Into nothing. It was Polly who prompted him to continue with his story.

'Safety in numbers, I suppose. So what happened next?'

'Nothing.'

'Nothing?'

'The story ended right there, with just a feeling of *needing* to travel south - to something better. A fresh start. Somewhere. The dreams and visions stopped, and stayed unresolved.'

'So, what did you do next?' she asked. 'After four days.'

'I headed back - back to our village - where they were waiting for me.'

'Who?'

'I told you. The elders. They knew I was coming so they'd prepared the final part of the ceremony.'

'What was that?'

'Oh, the usual. Making me lie in the sacred tipi while they burned sage and said prayers over me.'

'How long was that for?'

'Not entirely sure.' He chuckled as it all came back to him. 'That's when I got used to smoking the pipe big-time. I was barely conscious for most of it.'

'How did it end?'

'The elders gave me their prediction of how things would be for me from then on.'

'What were the 'things'? Were they right? Did it work?'

He chuckled again at her persistence for detail, before giving her an answer she wasn't expecting.

'I hope you're ready for this,' he began again.

'Ready for what?' He'd certainly got her attention.

'There was a girl travelling with us - with me - in our trek over the land bridge from the Asian continent, over the frozen sea and into what we now call Alaska.'

'But she wasn't real, was she?'

'Yes and no. But we were in love, that bit I do remember,' he replied, adding more to her confusion. 'My vision ended with that part sort of unresolved, but the elders, in their predictions after my fasting and isolation had been completed, gave me a quest.'

'What was it? This quest?'

'I had to search until I found the girl I'd travelled with in my journey over the ice,' he said, 'and not stop until then.'

Polly's next question was killing her - Hoping for one answer, but almost afraid to ask. But it didn't stop her.

'And...did you?'

'Find her, you mean? Or stop?' Was he deliberately exasperating her? To keep her guessing? Or was there something else?

'Maybe,' she thought, 'he went back to his first love.' She was bursting to know. 'Yes, goddammit!' she spluttered, out loud this time. '*Did* you find her?'

He paused. His next few words put her out of her misery although, at the same time, shocked her to such an extent that the breath was sucked out of her.

At least he was smiling when he finally answered.


'I'm looking at her.'

# Chapter Fifteen

'Do you think it right we should let Amitola and Polly go off into the wilderness? Alone?' asked Chumani, settling down Wanagi for his sleep after his feed.

'We?' questioned Red, turning down the sound on the country radio station. 'You mean *I* let them go? I thought it was your idea.' He thought for a while, then added, 'And you can hardly call it 'wilderness'. They're a day's ride away at most.'

'You know what I mean,' she said.

It was the 'alone' bit that troubled her.

Red made a vain attempt to reassure her. 'She's still in mourning. She has to be released from that, first. My uncle is fully aware. He's hardly going to try anything on with her.'

'That's not what worries me,' she admitted. 'It's Polly. Is *she* aware she has to be released before she...?'

The final words wouldn't come.

Red sighed. 'If something *does* happen, then it happens. They're both adults and it's not for us to interfere.'

'Then who should?' she asked. 'Who should...*look out* for her, I mean? She has no family. Not here, anyways.'

'She has us. She also has Ben and Sarah from the brewery if she does need help or a shoulder to....'

He hoped that would bring the conversation to an end.

He was wrong.

'Like I've already said, it's not Amitola I worry about,' she insisted. 'He knows our customs and, believe it or not, I trust him to stick by them. It's Polly. She's so vulnerable and probably *even she* doesn't know her own mind.

'Not while she's still grieving.'

He finally drew a line under the issue with, 'I'll talk to both of them when they get back,' turning up the sound on the radio as he did so. It was his favourite Tammy Wynette song.

Stand By Your Man.


As it turned out, he would be speaking to his uncle earlier than he expected. Red picked up the phone; Amitola was calling him from a gas station on the main highway.

He got straight to the point.

"You got that big-ass transporter gassed up?'

'How many you got?' Red guessed why he'd called. He needed help getting however many wild mustangs he'd caught, back to the Lazy B.

'I missed out on the stallion but this one mare, wait 'till you see her. She's a beauty - and two foals; twins, a filly and a colt. The colt alone willl more than make up for it.'

'What's your plan?'

'Your transporter should take *our* horses, including the pack-horse. The Cherokee and trailer should manage the mare and her young'uns.'

'Where are you?'

'At a diner just off 487 where it splits with 220. How long will you be?'

'Gimme an hour,' said Red. 'I'll bring Chumani to drive the mustangs, plus she'll be best at getting them boxed.'

Amitola hung up.

Red was right. His wife wasn't what was popularly soon to be known as 'a horse whisperer', but she really *could* communicate with all wildlings. Even bears and wolves. Polly had already witnessed this on a previous expedition into the grasslands when Joss was alive. She would easily calm the mare who, in turn, would instill that same lack of fear into her foals.

Two hours later they were headed back to the Lazy B - two horse boxes, six horses, two children (Chumani had left Wanagi with the cook's daughter back at the ranch), plus the four adults.

'I really appreciate this, nephew,' said Amitola as he opened the cold one Red handed him as they all piled into their respective truck cabins. 'I didn't relish keeping the foals safe from predators for another night, and on the journey home, on horseback.'

'You did the right thing,' agreed Red. 'Even twins are safe enough in the herd but alone with just you and Polly, out there, one could easily be picked off by a cougar. Even wolves.'

Amitola relaxed. He knew his nephew would be the one ultimately benefitting from the capture of the wild mustangs but, even so, he regarded it a favour that Red had so readily stepped up to get them all safely back to the ranch.

'Thanks, nephew,' he said, easing himself back into the comfort of a real seat after days in the saddle. He dozed.

Polly was less fortunate. She had to keep awake. She was paired with Chumani along with her daughter, Petal. Their son, Badger, was in with Red and Amitola. It gave Chumani the perfect opportunity to pick up on the conversation she'd had with Red the evening before - about Polly and Amitola, and whether they had a future together.

Chumani was clearly itching to ask Polly about that very thing. Her silence, combined with the furtive glances she gave Polly whenever it was safe to take her eyes off the road, became too much for Polly to bear. She could stand it no longer.

'What?' she asked, not knowing what to expect.

'Well?'

The brevity of Chumani's response was equally irritating.

'Well, what?' pressed Polly.

'How did you get on...?'

'We got a mare and two foals.'

'That's not what I meant.'

'Then what? What *do* you mean?'

'How did you get on with...you know?'

'Amitola? You're worried about Amitola?'

'Not worried, exactly.' Chumani was now trying to find the right words. 'Just...concerned, I guess. In case...'

'Nothing happened,' broke in Polly, heading off Chumani's clear intention to suggest that she and Amitola had - or *might* have - been carried away 'in the moment' whilst on some reckless escapade together. But it didn't ease things. Not quite.

'That's good to hear,' said Chumani, calmer now. But there were still unanswered questions. 'But, does that mean that you might...there might be...?'

'Yes. There's every chance we might.' Polly was agreeing to 'something' that neither of them had spelt out completely, but each of them knew exactly what they were talking about. Or thought they knew.

But what of Amitola? Did he even have a say in the outcome? Whatever it was? Chumani headed for safer ground. She changed the subject.

'Wanagi's been very good. He's almost dry.'

It was a good move on Chumani's part. Polly had missed her baby, so good news about him during the few days they had been apart - for the first time - was welcome.

Amitola *did* have an easier 'ride' with Red when it

came to the subject of '*how did you and Polly get on during the trip*.'

Much easier.

He ignored it. He decided to let his uncle sleep.

For one thing, Red considered it none of his business - nor that of Chumani's. For another, he figured, 'what does it matter'? He stood by his view that they were both adults and, in spite of some of the stories - about women - that Amitola came back with after his trips south every year, the situation with Polly was different.

He considered her to be family.

Amitola knew or at least sensed this too. Even so, his tribal instincts steeped in tradition embraced an unquestionable respect for a widow during her period of grieving. They - Amitola and Polly - had discussed the whole situation immediately after he'd described to her his vision and the prediction - the instruction - passed onto him by the elders in his tribe.

It seemed the natural thing to do.

The reality was that both of them felt the same attraction to each other but they were confident enough to wait. To wait for each other - to wait for each other to be ready to take things forward. The concept that the end to her mourning period had to be determined by another - usually the chief or elder within the family - was unfamiliar to her until Amitola explained it.

In the absence of a tribal leader, who would that 'other' be? Would she be locked in a state of limbo indefinitely, destined to grieve for Joss for ever? At that present time, or up to the point when Amitola had revealed his destiny, she was happy to do nothing. Again, up to that point a new relationship - with anyone - had not even been on her agenda.

Why should it be?

But now things were different. And they did wait.

Strange as it may seem, it was relatively easy for both of them. Amitola's revelation of his boyhood visions, and those he experienced later featuring the image of Polly, had opened up an imaginary door to a spiritual world they could share. Until then, any feelings Polly may have had for Amitola lay dormant, suppressed both by her recent loss as well as her focus on Wanagi.

For Amitola it was similar, albeit not exactly the same.

As soon as he'd laid eyes on Polly he'd recognised her as the same girl the elders had instructed him to find. He knew he'd reached the end of a journey. At last he could relax. It was destiny fulfilled, as prescribed for him by The Great Spirit and over which he had no say. Now nothing and no-one could change what may or may not unfold in the days to come. Days that could, if it was so destined, possibly turn into weeks, months or even years.

However, he realised it may not be quite as easy for Polly. How would she deal with the feelings they shared? With that in mind, he explained how a mutual love shared between two people such as themselves could withstand all challenges.

Even time.

'This was told to me by the elder, the shaman in our tribe,' he began. 'He predicted that, when I at last found the girl from my visions - you, Polly - that I would need to understand the *nature* of the love I could expect to experience.

'He said that you and I should learn to fly as high as we could, together, but without being *tied* together; not tethered. Only then could we expect our love to last, love based on duty, respect but without chains.

'Initially I found this idea difficult to comprehend, so I asked him to explain this in more detail. He said that when he was a young man, he and his betrothed were told by their wise man of the village to venture out and catch two wild birds; his soon-to-be bride was to capture a falcon, whilst he was to catch an eagle, bringing them both to him. They did so and he then told them to tie the two birds together.

'Naturally they tried to fly away but couldn't.

'That's when the secret of a good marriage began to unfold; to become clear. Being tied together as the two birds were, each frustrated the other's efforts to fly. After several attempts,  and each time falling helplessly to the ground, they started to peck at each other.

'Their shaman explained how the same destiny would await them, that they would turn on each other if they regarded their love as tying them both together, not allowing each other to fly as high as they could in complete freedom. Independently. It was a lesson well learnt resulting in the wise man and his wife living to a ripe old age - together - in relative harmony.'

Polly listened to the story and it made her feel better, more confident that nothing and no-one would come between them, if that was what the future held.

But she didn't have to wait long.

Her parents, Aran and Tara, had promised to visit each year and it was during their next stay at The Lazy B that Red explained the 'situation' in which Polly and, for that matter Amitola, found themselves. He suggested that in order for Polly to move forward she needed to be released from her state of mourning. Only then could she take up any new relationship, if she so wanted.

It therefore fell upon Aran to grant Polly that freedom. In some ways it might have proved more logical for it to rest on Joss' father, but his parents were in poor health and their trips to Wyoming were a thing of the past.

And so it was that Amitola's quest, as laid down by his elders some twenty five years previously, looked like coming to an end. Even so, there were no guarantees that the fulfillment of those prophesies would be without further challenges.

Both for him and for those around him.

# Chapter Sixteen

'I think we might have bear trouble again.'

Red's announcement came during the evening meal. He and Chumani had invited Polly and Amitola round for supper, given that it was a Saturday and, in theory, the next day was a rest day. It was the closest they all had to family. Each other.

'Again? I thought that grizzly looked after the herd, not threaten it.'

Amitola was, of course, referring to the bear affectionately called 'Young Bastard', the offspring of 'Old Bastard'. The latter was once a sworn enemy of Red's but everything changed when the grizzly protected him and his party during one overnight campout in the grasslands.

Old Bastard saw off a pack of timber wolves.

Young Bastard was seen later, some *years* afterwards, keeping sentry over the Lazy B's herds of buffalo and wild mustang. He often took his post standing guard on the high rise overlooking the meadow where they were grazing - the same spot where Jim and Clare, together with their faithful retainer, Seth, were buried.

And then Joss, of course.

It was a ritual the 'friendly' grizzly had kept up ever since - seemingly taking over from Old Bastard after *he* died.

Until recently, that was.

In the past week, during Red's last check on both herds just before sunset he sensed something. It made him uneasy; the feeling of being watched. But by whom? Or what? His stock sensed it too and displayed the same uneasiness you usually only get when they are being stalked. Red looked for the normal signs such as tracks, scat, or fur rubbed off on fence posts or wire. It wasn't until he saw the grizzly, just before the grizzly saw him and sloped off, that he was certain.

It wasn't Young Bastard.

He was explaining all this as his uncle listened intently. 'What made you so sure?' Amitola asked. 'It was getting dark, so how could you be certain.'

'He had this streak of white hair - fur - from his snout and going over to between his ears.'

'Like mine?' asked Badger.

'Not quite, son,' said Red. 'But close. There'd be no mistaking you.' The distinctive shock of white in his otherwise black hair, evident even at birth, had given him his name.

'Shall we go after him?' asked Amitola.

'I don't know,' Red replied. 'I'm hoping we don't have to. You know how much I hate killing wild animals, even those who pose a threat.'

'Maybe Young Bastard'll solve the problem for us...and chase him off,' Badger suggested.

'What have I told you about swearing, young man,' chided Chumani. 'Especially at the table.'

'But Mamma,' pleaded Badger, 'dad and uncle Amitola...'

'That's different,' Red said, without explaining why. Badger seemed to accept it. For now. But Red had to agree. 'You're right, son. Young B... - the bear - will hopefully come back to sort things so we don't have to.'

Young Bastard did return.

And nothing was seen of the other grizzly, at least not for a while. But what was more mysterious, and what puzzled both Red and Amitola most, was how the buffalo and mustang herds knew the *difference*. In fact, they would often appear restless and insecure until they knew Young Bastard was looking over them. Looking *after* them. It was widely accepted among the Lakota Sioux that bears provided guardianship and protection. But it was remarkable all the same that domesticated animals and potential prey should be able to distinguish between harmful and benign predators.

'Just make sure you stay close to the house as soon as it starts to get dark,' counselled Chumani to both their children, hoping to draw a line under the topic.

But it left them all with the same sense of unease.


At the end of each 'dude ranch' season, around Labor Day, it was the convention for Red and most of the staff members on that side of the ranch operation to go on a picnic out near the river. It was an annual treat and a way to say 'Thank You'. The previous owners and founders, Jim and Clare Schultz, had started the custom way back as far as Red could remember. He simply honored the tradition.

By that time, Amitola and Polly had sort of begun 'to see each other' as it were, keeping things low key despite Polly being released from her period of mourning. Although they hadn't moved in together, they still 'entertained each other' regularly in their respective cabins on the ranch. But what nobody seemed to associate was how the beginning of their relationship coincided with the first sightings of the rogue bear.

That would soon change.

The September sun was already hotting up when the staff party set out soon after breakfast. They headed for the river in buckboards and wagons - four in all - enough to carry food and cooking utensils as well as passengers. Red, Chumani, Polly and Amitola elected to ride alongside, as 'shotgun' you might say - or *have* said, some hundred years prior in the 'old' wild west. They were joined at a pre-appointed place north of the river by May-Belle and Cary Butler, their friends and neighbors from the ranch bordering The Lazy B.

The one thing they hadn't brought along - because they didn't need to - was wood for the fire. Amitola and Polly had volunteered to forage for that, setting out on foot to gather what they could once they struck camp. They were barely out of sight of the wagons as they ventured into nearby woods for signs of dead trees, when Polly stopped.

'Did you hear that?'

'Hear what? Amitola asked.

'Not quite a growl. More like heavy breathing.'

'Hey,' he chuckled, 'I know I'm feeling amorous, but I didn't think even *you* could hear me that time.'

'I'm being serious. Listen.'

He could tell when she wasn't joking. Like now.

'Maybe we should...' he began but, before he could finish the sentence, a big dark shape headed towards them.

Correction: headed towards *him*.

He'd experienced a wealth of similar situations after years living for weeks on end in the wild, and was always on the alert. Just in case. Now he switched to survival mode. Without having to think about it - for one thing he didn't have *time* to think - he figured he had two options. His knife, or his Colt. Dropping what kindling he had, he elected for both, but in a particular order. If he was lucky, he could sink his Bowie knife into the heart of the animal with fatal effect, whereas his Colt - unless he could fire off a series of rounds - might only wound the bear, at best.

On its own, the Colt was not ideal but, before he could do anything there was a cry, 'Stop!' from Polly.

Both Amitola - and the bear - froze.

Only then, with the bear poised and ready to strike but so startled by her command therefore stock still, did she recognise him. First it was the streak of white hair that gave him away but, most of all, it was the brilliance of the eyes. Like most bears, they should have been brown.

But they were blue.

'Joss?' she whispered, hardly able to get any words out.

'Is it really you?'

Amitola remained frozen, for once totally undecided *what* to do but also unsure that what he was seeing, and what he was about to witness, was indeed real. It was more like a scene from one of his hallucinatory journeys - *after a ton of peyote*. But he sensed that any immediate danger had miraculously passed. In sheer relief he exhaled audibly before dropping his arms to his side. He looked on, uncertain what would happen next.

And waited.

In the minutes - no, seconds - that followed, when it seemed everything was playing out in slow motion, he could hardly believe his own eyes. Years later after he had told and re-told the story so many times over and over, it still seemed incredible.

'Is it really you, darling?' she repeated, moving closer to the bear.

Those words were the trigger for what was about to happen as she gradually realised it *was* Joss. They were words that reached out to the husband she thought was dead; had been killed but now appeared to be alive again. But as what? His rage - the rage of the bear, or was it Joss - subsided. Wicasa-Mato - the Man-Bear - raised his arms to make his eight foot frame on two legs seem even greater. But he wasn't about to harm her. He slowly lowered himself to stand before her, now on all fours. As she continued to approach the bear, much to the fear and consternation of Amitola who could merely look on in amazement, it was the eyes of Joss - his blue eyes, softening - that assured her she had nothing to fear.

And nothing to lose.

She now had everything to gain - to reclaim.

'I've missed you *so* much,' she sobbed and, at that very point the mighty grizzly completed his transition into the husband she'd loved, and lost.

Her husband was alive again. As Joss. Reunited.

Or so it seemed. But his first words chilled her to the bone.

'I can't stay.'

Polly was sobbing uncontrollably now. Joss gathered her in his arms to console her, but to no avail. Not immediately. She clung onto him, her face buried in his neck, her fingers feeling the texture of the shirt he'd been wearing the last time she saw him alive. He really *was* there before her, even wearing the same clothes he'd worn on that last day.

It wasn't a dream, nor one of Amitola's visions.

This time it was real.

The bear, or rather Joss, cast a glance over to Amitola with a gesture that told him to remain calm, to holster his weapons. Without a word Amitola complied. After all, the very concept of a Wicasa-Mato - a Man-Bear - was all too familiar to him. He was amazed at how relaxed he now felt, strangely happy for Polly that she was reunited with the love of her life.

He walked alone back to the camp without looking back.

It was dawn the following day by the time Polly returned from the woods. Chumani was the first to greet her, her kind words never questioning events that may have unfolded in the hours during which she'd spent with her departed husband.

Precious hours spent alone with Joss yet again.

Amitola had described the events he'd witnessed the night before to Chumani, and to Red, knowing it was only half the story. He wouldn't press Polly for further detail.

At least not yet.

'You must be tired,' he said as he joined her by the coffee pot bubbling over the heat from the fire. He pondered the fact that the heat was from the same remains of the dry wood he'd collected as he returned from the woods the previous evening. She accepted his offer of the steaming cup of black liquid but set it down to cool before drinking. He waited for her to speak, to say something, even if it had nothing to do with the hours - the missing hours - since he'd last been with her. But she was bursting to share them with someone.

Who better, than with Amitola?

'He was in a lot of pain,' she said at last. 'Emotional pain.'

'He will be at peace now,' he reassured her. But how did *he* know that? She would discover later that Amitola was more than versed in how The Great Spirit guided our lives.

'Thank you.' She caught hold of the one hand free of his coffee cup, squeezing then releasing it in reply. But the tears flowed from her once more as she listened to what he was about to say, with a choice of words rationalising to her the irrational, explaining to her the inexplicable. She would never doubt any of the truth in his wild stories ever again, nor dismiss the wisdom hidden within his many tales.

'He was taken so soon, so suddenly, he didn't have a chance to say goodbye. The Great Spirit blessed him with that opportunity and a second chance for you to be together.'

Amitola paused for a while, then continued. 'Be assured he hasn't left you even now. He still rests in here.' With that, he placed his hand over his heart then pointed to his temple. 'And he will never leave you again. Not completely.'

'I'm sorry,' she said, gripping his hand once more.

'You don't have to be sorry. We - you and I - can still have *our* kind of love. We Lakota have ways to deal with these situations. We will talk later. Meanwhile, let me give you this.'

He reached for his pipe, taking one of the eagle feathers tied to the stem. He held it over her head first, before offering a blessing granting  bravery and happiness in Lakota words she understood.

Then he placed it in her palm.

'Keep this safe and it will keep you safe. You are Lakota in your heart and in your heritage so, unlike all white men, you are allowed to possess this sacred token. But, as I said, let us talk later.'


He was silent for the rest of the day.


### *The sanctity of the eagle; things you should know...*

*It is illegal for a white man to kill or even touch an eagle, dead or alive. If you stumble upon the carcass of a dead eagle, leave it alone. It is illegal for the white man to own an eagle feather. That privilege is the domain of* registered *Native American Indians however, even they cannot gift an eagle feather to any other than another registered member of a tribe.*

*Those who receive the gift of an eagle feather are blessed with gratitude, love and respect.*

*They bring good fortune to those honoured with an eagle feather and represent honesty, truth, majesty, strength, courage, wisdom, power and freedom.*

*They also bring spiritual and mental strength.*

# Chapter Seventeen

The annual Lazy B picnic had been another success, the permanent staff feeling like part of a family - now including those that worked on the serious side of ranching as well as the seasonal accomodation and field trips. It was how Jim and Clare had wanted it when they decided to diversify all those years ago. Red had respected tradition.

If anyone apart from Red and his family missed the presence of Polly the previous night, nobody mentioned it. But Amitola *did* miss her. He'd lay awake most of the night going over scenarios, second-guessing what might be going on between Polly and Joss. Torturing himself. Even a secret session on his sacred pipe, away from the main group, did nothing to pacify him or lull him into sleep. Instead he spent most of the night in an unsettled, waking sleep, imagining the reunion of Polly and Joss and wondering how it might affect her - and the two of them - when she returned.

That is... if she *did* return. Would things ever be the same?

Chumani couldn't sleep either, her mind overflowing as she speculated on events surrounding the re-appearance of Amitola. Her first instinct was to look in on Polly again and, this time, press her for details of what had really transpired during the 'missing hours' - the time between Amitola leaving her alone the night before, and Polly turning up at the camp the next day. Careful not to disturb Red she snuck out of her bedroll and, instead, decided to seek out Amitola. But where had he gone? He wasn't in the main camp. She found him, thanks to the light of his own fire. He'd chosen a spot just beyond earshot of the main camp where he'd decided to salvage some solitude. His blanket lay over him, close to a small fire he'd built for his own personal comfort. But now he was glad of the company.

He was pleased it was Chumani.

'You understand these things better than your husband, my beloved nephew, so I will tell you what happened leading up to when I returned alone last evening.'

'In your own time and only if you need to,' she said unconvincingly. Much to Amitola's amazement she reached for the pipe he'd just filled with his special mixture.

'I didn't know you...'

'I don't,' she said before he could finish. 'But this is a special occasion, so don't tell Red.' With that she took a deep tug at the sacred pipe whilst Amitola looked on in astonishment, marvelling at the fact that she didn't choke.

She exhaled slowly, allowing him to continue his account.

'We saw Joss,' he began. 'Or, at least we saw the Wicasa-Mato - the Man-Bear - before he transitioned *into* Joss. I would have killed him, had Polly not shouted and stopped me.'

'Didn't you recognise him? The Bear? Or Joss?'

'It was the one we now call the rogue bear. The one that had recently appeared and, apparently, chased Young Bastard away. Just for a while, anyways.' Amitola took another toke on his pipe before continuing, handing it back to Chumani. It seemed to be having the desired effect; she appeared calmer. Amitola let his story unfold slowly, watching to see how she reacted.

'Like Red described him, he had this white streak from his muzzle and over his head. But we hadn't reckoned on the next revelation. Not at first. I noticed it just as he charged me.'

'What was it?'

'His eyes. They were blue, just like...'

'Joss' eyes,' said Chumani. It was the first striking feature she'd noticed about Joss the first time he came to the ranch for his ride-outs with Polly. That and his blond hair.

'Thank goodness Polly cried out in time. I could see he was headed for me, ready for the kill, but Polly stopped him in his tracks. Me too. We both froze. Me *and* the bear.'

'You said he changed into Joss. How did that happen?'

Amitola cleared his throat, the whole atmosphere had become emotionally charged as he relived the events, and as the same sensations of the encounter came flooding back to him.

'His face changed first, the shape of the head as well as the fur and hair and stuff. Then the fur on his body seemed to, like, melt away to be replaced by normal clothes. They must have been those he had on when he was shot.

'Come to think of it, I'm sure the shirt was torn and ripped around the shoulder where he'd taken the blast. Next to his heart. I didn't remember that until afterwards.'

'Did they talk?' she asked.

'If they did I couldn't hear what they said. They just whispered to each other. And embraced. That's when I left.'

Chumani and Amitola just sat, smoking and thinking but not talking. She had no more questions and, in any case, the rest was probably best left to her imagination. She didn't need to know. It was a private moment and, if Polly wanted to talk about it later, she would.


Chumani had retold Amitola's account to Red in as much detail as she could remember, no small thanks to the pipe she'd shared. She embellished the account with extra speculation of her own, adding details of what might have gone on *after* Amitola had left the scene that night.

Polly had returned, Red saw her but didn't speak. She did suspect he *knew* what had happened - leastways as far as things to which she knew his uncle had been witness. In the typical Lakota Sioux fashion, however, Red had been brought up to know when to remain silent, and when it was appropriate to ask questions. This was the rule of law - etiquette - when among strangers and, although he and Polly counted each other as friends, he recognised that this particular occasion called for extra dignity and respect to his friend. He should allow her the freedom of silence until she was ready. Or, as was usually the case, he would be patient and simply wait for Chumani to find out the full story and tell him.

That time came soon enough, not long after the party had returned to the ranch to settle back into daily routines. But there was still the potential situation regarding the ongoing affect the rogue bear - or so he was still being called - might have on the safety of their herds, if he ever came back.

They waited.

Two months went by and there was still no sign.

Instead, Young Bastard had returned to sentry duty on his familiar spot near to the graves where Jim, Clare, Seth and more recently Joss, had been buried. All seemed well with everyone prepared to hunker down for another harsh Wyoming winter. Thankfully, the snows held off until October, enabling the ranch hands to 'take care of business' between the end of the vacation season and the first of the bad weather. They were busy mending fences and roofs and ensuring there was plenty of winter feed stored before the harshness began to bite.

Amitola and Polly continued to see each other purely as friends, close friends, but it was a deep, platonic friendship. The strange - but welcome - factor in all this was that their feelings had strengthened since Polly's encounter with Joss that final time. There dependance and trust in each other had  intensified rather than softened *because of it*. It had afforded them both a kind of certainty and mutual understanding. It is said that a Lakota Sioux's love and act of marriage is based on *duty* towards his wife, although that isn't to say that it's a duty without feeling.

Furthermore, there is also the custom where, say, when a husband dies then it becomes the duty - the responsibility - of his brother to marry the widow after a respectful period of mourning. That was the position Amitola assumed towards Polly, even in the absence of actual marriage or the physical act that followed. But he knew that Polly would always carry undying love for Joss, unreservedly and without fail.

That never changed.


So it was no surprise that Amitola was among the first to learn of Polly's happy news one evening over supper. They were with Red, Chumani and their family when Polly just came out with it, without even warning Amitola.

'I'm going to have a baby.'

She looked round for reaction as soon as the words left her.

It was smiles all round, but Amitola was the first to speak.

'No need to ask who the father is.'

'Joss,' whispered Chumani. It was also no mystery to the rest of them, especially not to Polly, who turned to Amitola.

'Thank you. Thank you, Amitola. The power of the eagle feather has without doubt brought me happiness again and all because of you.'

She bent forward to kiss him lightly on the cheek.

'I hardly had anything to do with it,' he laughed, but realised he had to be just a little clearer. 'At least, not in the way you all might think.' They knew what he was really trying to say and they respected him for it.

'It was The Great Spirit,' he added for the absence of doubt.

That was enough to draw a line under the subject before more could be said. In any case, by that time they had all received one account or another, from someone or another, regarding 'the bear incident'and Polly and Amitola at the staff outing. Enough to satisfy the curiosity of Chumani anyway.

But it was Red who came up with the next revelation.

'I saw him again yesterday.'

'Saw who, Red?' Amitola had to ask, but he

wasn't surprised when the answer came back.

'The bear. The grizzly with the white stripe.'

'Sure it wasn't Young Bastard, nephew?'

'It was light this time, so yes. It was him alright. Out near the high ground over by the cemetary.'

'D'you intend doing anything about it?' asked Amitola.

'We don't need to,' broke in Polly. 'He's fine.' Her tone was terse, prickly, a hint of panic in her voice.

'Well, *he* may be fine. But what about the herd? How are they taking it? Have you thought of that?' Red wasn't used to others taking decisions when it involved his stock's safety.

'You have to trust me, Red,' said Polly and, with that, she excused herself and left the table. 'I'll be gone for a while.'

She gathered her coat and headed for the door. Amitola rose to go with her but she raised her hand, signalling she wanted to be on her own. 'I just need some air,' she said, and left.

Amitola sat back down but was uneasy, repeatedly glancing across at the door she'd just left by, finishing his beer in one series of swallows but then playing with the empty bottle, irritating his nephew until his fidgeting became too much.

'Go and see what she's up to if it bothers you that much,' said Red, a sense of resignation in his voice.

Amitola didn't actually need Red's permission, but he took it that it was OK to follow her out. He grabbed his coat, muttering something about being back soon as he, too, disappeared into the darkness outside.

It was one of those cool Wyoming nights when the northerly breeze down from Canada chilled the air, causing you to turn up your collar and sink lower into your coat for warmth. He looked across to Polly's cabin for any sign that she was home but there were no lights on. He listened for any sound of her but there was none, nor any moon to help him spot her in the dark fringes around the ranch where, he assumed, she might have taken a stroll to clear her head.

Nothing; not until the clouds parted to let the light through from a thin moon, just bright enough to send its beam over the high ground and home to the cemetary.

There she was.

Or, rather, there they were; Polly...and Joss.

Amitola could tell by his tall, lean frame it was Joss and, if that wasn't enough, in the moonlight he could just make out his blond hair. He and Polly were holding each other close, talking softly, until Joss pulled away - just far enough from her so he could reach out to pass his hand lovingly over where the unborn child nestled inside her.

His, *Joss'*, unborn child.

It was all Amitola needed or, indeed, wanted to see. He was sure now that Polly was in safe hands; in a good place. Silently and before his presence could be discovered by the couple, he made his way back to the main house.

It was time for a smoke. This time alone.

Later in the spring of the following year Polly gave birth to a healthy baby girl. She was born with a shock of dark brown hair, just a little lighter than her own black colour, and graced with her mother's unmistakable brown skin.

But her eyes were bright blue.

Polly called her 'Wohpe'.

*"More beautiful than any other."*

~ \*\*\* THE END...of the beginning \*\*\* ~

# Epilogue

The last thing I want is to create is a political storm. As an emerging author and not one who graces the bestseller lists - yet - I consider any influence I may have to be insignificant.

However, I do hope that this novel, as well as '*Wild Hearts Roam Free*' that preceded it, encourages you to take *some* time to read about the plight of The Native American Indian. Their circumstances and fate at the hands of the American government during and since the 1800s are shocking.

That's all I feel qualified to say on the matter, to make you aware, apart from applauding those among these noble races - especially young people - who have, and still are, aspiring to greater things. They achieve this through education as well as using the meaningful opportunities that remain out there, courtesy of the same American government; albeit years later.

On another topic, I must share the story my father told me related to all this, that I have never forgotten.

In the late 1800s, Chief Sitting Bull - for many regarded as one of the most significant and inspirational leaders of the Sioux Nation - came to England. Although technically a prisoner of the American army, he was granted leave to join Buffalo Bill Cody's Wild West Show.

The show included a tour to South West England.

During his short time as a celebrity in the show, apparently he became disenchanted and was most critical of the English, who paid their shilling to see him and his braves perform.

I hope that disillusionment didn't include my great grandfather and his son. They owned and ran a tailor's shop at 10, The Parade, Exmouth on the south coast of Devon; the town where my father was born.

He told me that Chief Sitting Bull actually visited the shop and met his grandfather Henry and his father, Albert Morey. More than that I have no details - nor proof - but, hey, if you can't believe your own father, then who can you believe?

That is my connection, albeit tenuous, to one of the greatest Lakota Sioux who ever lived, and who met presidents and kings. It was but well after he'd despatched General Custer.

But my sadness at what happened to Native Americans after the Battle of Greasy Grass (aka Little Bighorn) won't go away.

Why should I care?

*Why shouldn't I?*

# Other books by J S Morey

**WILD HEARTS ROAM FREE**

If you enjoyed *Wild Hearts Come Home* you will also love this companion novel. It, too, features Red and Chumani but also a young couple over from England, Eric and Maggie.

The Lazy B around which events take place, was actually founded by a German man and wife, Jim and Clare Schultz. They emigrated from a small Leicestershire village just after the Second World War.

It also features encounters with local wildlife, principally bears, wild mustang and wolves. You are also introduced to mystical folklore from the Lakota Sioux culture, including the legend of the White Buffalo Calf Woman.

The backdrop is again the wonderful state of Wyoming.

**THOSE ITALIAN GIRLS**

Make sure a trip to Tuscany is on your bucket list.

Meanwhile you can enjoy a virtual visit courtesy of this coming of age tale with injections of first love, a search for lost parents, and a murder mystery - all in one package.

And you get to meet 'those Italian girls'.

**READ MY SHORTS**

This selection of poems and short stories offers

thought-provoking writing to dip into when you're in the mood for a light read. But there is no lack of depth in the characterisations and plots, capped by a final section, memoir-style, depicting life in a small Leicetsershire village in the 1950s-60s.

### WOOD-SPIRIT

This brief anthology celebrates a variety of trees in verse, paying homage to their significance, meaning, properties and the stories surrounding them.

Illustrated or non-illustrated editions: your choice.

### LOVE SHOULD NEVER BE THIS HARD

Something to get your teeth into: a series of four separate stand-alone novels combined to make a saga-length set of romantic adventures. It spans some hundred years, beginning in the mid-1800s.

Books 1-4 include: *The Sign of the Rose; The Black Rose of Blaby; Rose:The Missing Years*; and *Finding Rose*.

There is a mystical theme throughout, centering on a Romani family and those who enter their lives. Some come with less than good intent but, over-all, each offers feel-good fiction and happy endings as tragedy and adversity are overcome.

With a variety of locations visited along the way you are treated to a journey from Southern Ireland to Devon and Cornwall, up to Leicestershire before returning to the westcountry.

For the mature reader they are a chance to go back

*WILD HEARTS COME HOME - Page 217*

in time to, some say, a better 'place'; for all ages there is are generous helpings of fact, actual events and locations woven into fictional accounts based, in parts, to real-life experiences.

**UNRESOLVED?**

This short story fills a gap in *Wild Hearts Roam Free*, but can still be enjoyed as an independent read. Featuring the same main characters, Eric and Maggie - on honeymoon - they include a murder mystery during their two-weeks in St Ives.

**For more information on the above and to keep pace with new books as they are published, visit *newnovel.co.uk*.**

Printed in Great Britain
by Amazon